"I'm not very good at faking it."

"Try!"

She shrugged resignedly and did as he asked, sliding her arms up around his neck, shocking herself when a shudder of sensation reverberated all through her as her fingertips brushed the warm flesh above his collar.

"Relax," he growled. "Let yourself go."

Do what he says, she ordered herself.... Pretend he loves you, wants you. Your dancing together is a prelude to a night of mad passion, the fulfillment of all your dreams.

Her whole body sank into his, her hips swaying more invitingly against his. Her mouth finally encountered and nibbled at an earlobe.

"Hell," he muttered, totally unprepared for his body's reaction to her seduction.

MIRANDA LEE grew up in New South Wales, Australia. She had a brief career as cellist in an orchestra, and then another as a computer programmer. A move to the country after marriage and the birth of the first of three daughters limited her career opportunities to being a full-time wife and mother. Encouraged by her family, she began writing in 1982. She favors a well-paced what-happens-next kind of story, but says what matters most "is that my books please and entertain my readers, leaving them feeling good and optimistic about love and marriage in our present topsy-turvy world."

Books by Miranda Lee

HARLEQUIN PRESENTS
1362—AFTER THE AFFAIR
1419—AN OBSESSIVE DESIRE
1481—THE RELUCTANT LOVER
1589—SCANDALOUS SEDUCTION
1651—A DATE WITH DESTINY

Miranda LEE

A Daring Proposition

Harlequin Books

TORONTO • NEW YORK • LONDON
AMSTERDAM • PARIS • SYDNEY • HAMBURG
STOCKHOLM • ATHENS • TOKYO • MILAN
MADRID • WARSAW • BUDAPEST • AUCKLAND

ISBN 0-373-11664-0

A DARING PROPOSITION

CHAPTER ONE

SAMANTHA stood in front of the large black desk, feeling sick with nerves. Her wide hazel eyes were fixed on the man seated behind the desk, on his darkly elegant head as it bowed to read the letter she had given him only moments before.

Impossible to gauge what his exact reaction to her resignation would be. But Guy Haywood had been her boss for five years and Samantha knew him far too well to hope to get off lightly in this matter.

His right index finger was tapping with apparent nonchalance on the desk as he appeared to re-read the letter. Any second now, she thought with increasing trepidation. Any second...

His chin came up slowly, his tanned and very handsome face dominated by piercing blue eyes. 'Is this your idea of a joke, Sam?' His voice was rich and very male, like the rest of him. 'Might I remind you that April Fool's Day was *last* week?'

'It's no joke, Guy,' she said with a composure that belied the butterflies in her stomach.

Again he looked at her with a bemused air. 'You *really* want to leave?' His tone suggested that such an event was impossible.

Oh, God, she thought despairingly. Of course I don't really want to leave. I love you, you fool. Can't you see that? Haven't you ever noticed?

She smothered a sigh. Of course he hadn't noticed. Why should he? She hadn't realised it herself till a year after coming to work for him, a wee bit late to start batting her eyelashes and giving him the come-on. Not that such a tack would have worked.

By then Samantha knew exactly what sort of woman her swinging bachelor boss was attracted to. She had to be blonde, preferably petite, definitely slender to the point of anorexic. If she had a brain, he didn't like it to be too much on display when in his company. Above all, she had to realise that his relationship with her was only semi-permanent and strictly sexual. Marriage and family commitments were not part of Guy Haywood's life plan.

As a statuesque brunette who couldn't bear to act dumb and wanted one day to marry and have children, Samantha had to accept she didn't quite fit the bill.

She should have left straight away once she had realised the awful truth, but love had a way of making one weak, and she'd hung in there, half hoping that during one of Guy's brief celibate stints between affairs he might notice what was right under his nose, might even change his mind about what he wanted in life.

Four years had gone by. Four years and a good few blondes.

Nothing had changed.

Nothing was *ever* going to change!

Her spine straightened.

'Yes,' she lied determinedly. 'I really want to leave.'

He leant back in the black leather swivel chair, his elbows on the aluminium arm rests, fingertips meeting at chest level. His eyes never left her. Light blue and clear as a cloudless spring sky, they had a range of expressions from charming to chilling.

Samantha did not feel charmed at that moment.

'Why?' he asked in that ultra-reasonable tone he adopted when he was at his most annoyed and trying to control it. Guy valued self-control above all else. It was the reason he had hired her in the first place, claiming that he liked her countrified air of no-nonsense down-to-earth practicality. He had wanted no female hysterics in *his* office!

Well, this practical, down-to-earth female did a highly emotional thing, she wanted to fling at him. She fell in love with her boss! Don't you find that hysterical?

'I've decided to go back home to live,' she stated calmly.

His face showed he didn't believe her, not for a minute. 'You *want* to go back to Paddy's Plains to live?' he scoffed. 'To a bush town with a population of one hundred and thirteen from which you were only too happy to escape?'

For a second Samantha regretted all those coffee breaks they had shared when he had elicited far too much of her background. Paddy's Plains wasn't quite as small as he suggested, but it wasn't much bigger. As a teenager she'd had to travel twenty miles to the next town to go to high school. Naturally, Guy would be suspicious of her wanting to go back to a life she'd admitted finding much too narrow and which offered her no employment opportunity other than serving behind the counter in her parents' general store. But it was the only excuse she could think of.

She took a deep breath and let it out evenly. 'Yes,' she said. 'I need a break. I'm tired of the rat race. I'm tired of Sydney.'

'Then take a week off.'

He wasn't going to let her quit, she thought with a wild mixture of panic and pleasure.

Don't you dare weaken, an inner voice berated. You'll regret it. Remember dear, sweet Debra yesterday? Long blonde hair, eyes like limpid pools, as slender as a willow branch. Guy's taking her out tonight to dinner and a show. They made plans in this very office, in front of you. Will you be able to stand it when he gives up smoking again tomorrow, as he does every time he starts a new affair? You've stood it for far too long, dying inside every time it happens. Soon you'll be *dead*!

Her teeth clenched hard in her jaw. 'A week won't do it,' she countered tautly. 'Besides, I——'

'If it's money, you can have a raise,' he cut in coldly.

'It's not money,' she returned, the beginnings of fluster sending heat into her cheeks. Oh, why couldn't he let her resign with dignity?

He snapped forward on the chair, the action sending a lock of his dark brown hair on to his high wide forehead. He scooped it back with an angry sweep of his hand and set exasperated eyes upon her. 'Damn it all, Sam!' he pronounced, angry now and showing it for once. 'You and I know that this job is your life almost as much as it's mine. You don't want to go back to that tinpot town. You're a city girl now. A career girl. You'd go mad out there in the bush. You'd be bored to tears within days!'

He stood up then and strode around the desk, putting firm hands on her shoulders and turning her to face him. Her whole insides tightened, as they did whenever he touched her, even accidentally.

'Sam,' he said in a voice so unexpectedly tender that it brought a lump to her throat, 'take some time off, if that's what you want, but please...' his lips pulled back in a smile designed to melt any woman's heart '... don't desert the ship. You're my first mate, and this captain needs you.'

That almost did it. Telling a woman that you needed her was almost as persuasive as saying you loved her.

But not quite.

'No, Guy.' Samantha swallowed down the lump and lifted her chin. 'I've given you two months' notice, plenty of time to break in someone new so that I can leave without any hitches. If you like I'll ask Mrs Walton if she's interested. I know she wants to work somewhere full-time, and she's already familiar with the layout here.'

Guy's hands dropped from her shoulders and he fairly scowled. 'That stupid woman is hard pushed to answer the phone. She's a complete ditherbrain!'

'No, she's not,' Samantha defended. 'She's very intelligent. Have a heart, Guy. She's been out of the work-force for years and only had a few weeks re-training before the agency put her on as a temp. I felt very sorry for her getting someone as demanding as you for a boss on her first job. You frightened the life out of her. If I hadn't *had* to go home for my brother's wedding that week I wouldn't have.'

'Pity you did!' he grumbled. 'The place was a mess by the time you got back. That woman couldn't possibly do your job on a regular basis. You're more than a secretary, dammit. You're my personal assistant, my right-hand man, my... Hell, Sam, I can't do without you!' he announced in an aggrieved tone.

'No one's indispensable,' she returned quietly.

He glared at her calm demeanour, then spun away to stalk back to his chair, more agitated than Samantha had ever seen him before.

But there was no real satisfaction in having disturbed his equilibrium for once. He was temporarily put out, that was all. Irritated that his well-run ship was sailing into some rough weather for a while. But in the end he would survive, would go on as though she had never made a single wave in his life.

The pain of it all was a knife twisting in Samantha's heart. Loving someone who didn't love you back, who wasn't even aware of you as a member of the opposite sex, was sheer torture.

'Well, you've certainly picked a fine time to leave me in the lurch,' he muttered as he glared up at her once more. 'I've just booked the Dambusters for an Australian tour next summer. You know how much organising goes into a tour for a popular rock band like that. They want to make a music video while they're here as well, something I was going to discuss with you at a later date, but...'

He shrugged, looking oddly lost, and Samantha almost weakened.

But only almost.

'I'll still be here for two months,' she reasoned. 'Plenty of time to make all the bookings for the tour. And, since you won't consider Mrs Walton, I'll let the head-hunters know you're on the look-out for a new secretary.'

'I don't want a new secretary,' he growled, sounding and looking like a sulky little boy.

Samantha almost laughed as she watched his bottom lip pout slightly, his very sexy bottom lip. It was hard to believe at times that he was thirty-six, he was so young-looking, with very few lines around his eyes and mouth. But then, a man was always a boy, her mother had used to say, till he became a father. Something *this* particular male would go to great pains to avoid, Samantha thought drily.

Guy spotted her cynical amusement, and immediately any hint of boyishness disappeared, replaced by the implacable face of the man who hadn't become a highly successful showbiz agent and entrepreneur by being soft.

He picked up her letter of resignation and ripped it asunder, depositing the pieces in the waste-paper basket beside him. 'Let's not hear any more of this nonsense, Sam,' he pronounced belligerently. 'You've made your point. I've been working you too hard. Take a fortnight off starting next Monday and there'll be another five grand a year in your pay-packet as from today.'

Samantha was taken aback for a moment. This type of bullying, high-handed tactic was not one Guy ever used with his business associates. He usually got his way with either cool logic or latherings of charm. He was never aggressive. Aggression, he'd always claimed, bred aggression.

It certainly did in this case.

She drew herself up straight and glared at him. 'I don't think I *have* made my point. *You* certainly haven't got it, anyway! Two months, Guy,' she bit out. 'Tear up another letter of mine like that and it will be two minutes, tour or no bloody tour!'

She had the satisfaction of seeing Guy literally gape at her. The prim and proper Miss Samantha Peters, *swearing*? His cool, calm and collected secretary, losing her temper? Unheard of!

If she'd had her hair loose she could have tossed her head as she turned to make a dramatic exit. As it was, with her long brown waves tamed into her usual coiled bun, she had to settle for swinging on her sensible heels and marching out of his office into hers, pulling the intervening door shut with a resounding bang.

Guy made no attempt to follow her or call her back. Running after tantrum-throwing secretaries was not his style.

Samantha was shaking when she finally sat down at her own desk. Literally shaking.

You've done the right thing, she kept telling herself. The only thing. You couldn't have gone on indefinitely, trying to hide your feelings, putting up with the agony of his indifference just to savour the dubious pleasure of his company. It was self-destructive and demeaning. It was . . . futile.

Yes, she decided with a shuddering sigh. You've done the right thing.

Sixty seconds later she was in her private wash-room, bawling her eyes out.

The traffic crawled across the bridge the following morning, bumper to bumper. Samantha checked her watch, accepted she would probably be late, then turned her head to gaze resignedly through the window of the bus down at the harbour below.

Not quite postcard material today, she thought wearily as another squall of rain dumped itself on Sydney. Really, wasn't it *ever* going to stop raining?

It was cold too. Far too cold for April. Anyone would think it was the dead of winter, instead of mid-autumn.

She rubbed a circle on the window to clear the mist on the glass, and could just make out the opera house in the distance. It looked uncustomarily dismal and grey, the sails of its roof huddling on Benelong Point like wet droopy birds. Closer in, a ferry chugged to a halt at the quay, spilling darkly raincoated people out on to the wet pier.

Samantha sighed. How depressing it all looked. Which was the last thing she needed this morning. The only consolation to having to face another day with Guy was that it was Friday. She really needed two days away from him.

Yesterday had proved to be a dreadful strain. He had called her back into the office eventually, but he hadn't tried to talk her out of leaving. Instead he had made a surprising apology, then insisted they go through all the files together, checking on every person, act or group that he managed, seeing what they were doing at that moment and what could be lined up for them in the immediate future. His attitude had been matter-of-fact and businesslike. Clearly he had accepted the situation and wanted to get the ship shipshape before his 'first mate' set off for other horizons.

His easy acceptance of her leaving upset Samantha terribly. So did their meticulous going through the files. With each file memories were thrown up to her, memories that held a disturbing amount of recalled pleasure.

How could she have forgotten that her life over the past five years had been filled with all sorts of exciting and rewarding events? What about the shows she had been to that involved singers and musicians Guy had managed? The premières, the parties afterwards? What of all the interesting, larger-than-life people she had met? The challenges she had had to rise to? The satisfaction she had felt when something she had personally organised had gone off without a hitch?

When she left Haywood Promotions she would leave not just Guy, but a way of life. What would she do? Where would she go?

Oh, she didn't doubt she could get another job in Sydney, but could she bear to be in the same city as the man she loved and not be a part of his life? Guy was a high-profile personality. He would be on television, in newspapers and magazines, probably with a stunning blonde in tow.

Samantha grimaced, remembering his date with Debra last night. She was a relatively successful singer on the local club circuit who had come to Guy, ostensibly seeking him as a new manager. One hour after walking into his life she had looked like becoming his next lover.

Would she have gone to bed with Guy on their first date? Samantha wondered bitterly.

Nothing surer, came back the cruel answer.

Her heart squeezed tight.

'Excuse me, but don't you get out here?'

Samantha jolted out of her mental agony, throwing the woman seated next to her a startled look before recognising her as a regular on this particular bus. Her eyes snapped back to see that they had long left the bridge and were standing at the King Street junction. Luckily the lights were red at that moment so the bus couldn't move off.

'Gosh, yes, I do,' Samantha gasped, snatching up her umbrella and jumping to her feet. 'Thank you so much.'

'No trouble. You'd better hurry, though. The lights will change soon.'

They did. Just as Samantha made it to the back platform. The bus lurched forward and she half jumped, half fell off, landing in a gutter that was doing a good imitation of the Grand Canyon rapids in full flood.

It was all she could do to keep her balance as the torrent surged around her ankles, splashing up her legs and under her skirt. She swayed and yelped. People were streaming by along the pavement, shoulders hunched, heads down, umbrellas jammed down low. But no one stopped to help. No one cared.

'Who could ever want to live in this heartless place?' she muttered, and stomped out of the raging torrent, unleashing her automatic umbrella with a vicious snap.

You do, came the dampening answer.

Infuriated with herself more than the rain, Samantha joined the trampling herd and eventually made it across George and Pitt Street, up through Martin Place then left down Elizabeth Street to the building that housed Guy's office. The rain eased off as soon as she pushed through the circular glass doors, making her mutter several reproachful words to higher authorities.

Not that *He* would take any notice, Samantha thought crossly. Look at all the prayers she had said on a certain other matter! She might as well have been praying to win the lotto, for all the results she'd had.

Soaked and very irritated, Samantha marched across the huge black and white tiled foyer and stuffed herself into one of the crowded lifts, jabbing the floor-fourteen button with the end of her umbrella. Living in the city, she decided, wasn't conducive to maintaining the sweet, Christian-like nature she'd had as a child.

We-ll, she rethought more honestly as the lift heaved its cargo upwards, one shuddering floor at a time. Perhaps I never was exactly sweet...

The memory of herself at high school flooded back, bringing with it the remembered agony of her adolescence. On the surface she had maintained the quiet, reserved, ladylike façade that her mother's strict country upbringing had imparted to her. Underneath she had longed to break out, to scream at her classmates who had cruelly nicknamed her Amazon Sam, to rant and rave against the body Mother Nature had given her. No wonder she and poor skinny, pimply Norman had gravitated towards each other. They had been the misfits in their class. The uglies.

Samantha smiled wryly to herself in the corner of the lift as she thought of her graduation dance. She'd looked as good as she could that night, all done up and dressed in a pretty mauve dress that had minimised her figure faults. Norman had looked surprisingly good as well, his well-tailored suit giving him shoulders, the night-light softening the effect of his bad skin.

Had it been her improved appearance or the promise of imminent freedom from the torture of school that had made her act so recklessly later in the evening?

Samantha sighed as floor nine came and went. Be honest, she told herself. You know precisely why you let Norman go "all the way". He started telling you you were beautiful and that he loved you.

Now, no other boys had ever said either of those things to Samantha. At five feet ten inches tall and carrying far too many pounds during her teenage years, she had not been the *femme fatale* of her school.

Norman's protestations of ever-lasting love had been very disarming.

Only later had Samantha realised what a crazy thing she had done, giving her virginity so carelessly. She hadn't even enjoyed it! Could hardly even remember it happening, it had been over so fast. Never again, she had vowed. Never again!

It had been difficult, though, to convince Norman she didn't love him, and it had been a relief when at the end of summer she had gone to live with her widowed Aunt Vonnie in far-away coastal Newcastle while she did a secretarial course.

Samantha shook her head fondly as she thought of her Aunt Vonnie. It had been her aunt who had directed her towards more sensible eating habits, which had trimmed down her bulk to more graceful proportions, her aunt who had paid for her deportment lessons, her aunt who'd overridden parental objection when she'd wanted to find a career in Sydney.

Samantha had been ever so grateful to her at the time. Now she wasn't so sure. If she hadn't come to Sydney, hadn't answered that newspaper advertisement which had ended up with her sharing a flat with gorgeous blonde Lana, hadn't met Guy that ghastly night when Lana had been supposed to go to *Jesus Christ Superstar* with him and stood him up...

'Don't you get out here?' someone said for the second time that day.

Samantha bit her lip and muttered sheepish thanks to the man holding the doors open for her. This would never do, she told herself as she squelched along the green-carpeted corridor. What did it matter what she'd done all those years ago or how she'd come to be in Sydney in the first place?

Her problem was getting through today, through having to watch Guy breeze in all bright-eyed and bushy-tailed, without a cigarette in sight.

She stopped at the door furthest along on the left and fished around in her handbag for her set of office keys. Finding them, she inserted the heaviest one, turned the lock and extracted the key. She was about to go in when she stopped and stared at the gilt lettering on the door. 'HAYWOOD PROMOTIONS,' it said on the top line. 'GUY HAYWOOD—MANAGING DIRECTOR.'

She could vividly recall the day they had moved into this office, the feeling of excited relief at having a real place to work in after many difficult months of trying to help Guy run his expanding business from the front room of his terraced house in Paddington.

He had taken her out to dinner after work as a reward for staying on late. Tired and hungry, she had gone, without thinking of any possible consequences.

Not that Guy hadn't been a perfect gentleman. He had. But it had been the first time Samantha had been exposed to the relaxed, social animal her boss became during his leisure hours, so different from the demanding, often distracted dynamo she dealt with during the day.

She'd always thought him attractive, admiring his elegant dark looks as well as his tall, athletic build. But she had never before felt the impact of his sex appeal, which had hit her in waves from across the table as he'd automatically slipped into the mode of charming dinner companion. He hadn't realised what effect he was having on her, she was sure, but by the end of the night her feelings had taken an irreversible change of direction, her respectful admiration being overwhelmed by a love that was to grow deeper and deeper with the passing of time.

Controlling a rush of emotion, Samantha opened the door and went inside, shutting the door quickly behind her. She leant against it for a moment, then looked up at the clock on the far wall. Five past nine. Not too late. Still plenty of time to get herself under control and organised before Guy made his usual appearance somewhere between nine-thirty and ten.

She would have to hurry, though, and dashed a rebel tear from her cheek. She didn't want to look flustered or upset when Guy arrived. She wanted to be every inch her usual competent self. All she could salvage from this situation was her pride and, by golly, she was going to leave here with it intact.

Taking a deep breath, she walked briskly across the reception area, dumping her handbag on her chair before continuing on into the small room which doubled as a kitchenette-store-room. There, she propped her umbrella in a corner, hung her raincoat on a wall peg, then stripped off her wet tights and shoes, replacing them with spares she kept in an old filing cabinet.

Once the kettle was on the boil for a much needed cup of coffee she went into the adjoining wash-room to make repairs to her face and hair.

The reflection that confronted Samantha would not have won cover-girl of the year. But neither would it have got the wooden spoon award for looks. She had good skin and a balanced bone-structure, clear hazel eyes, a straight nose, well-shaped lips and an elegant neck, shown to perfection by the way she always wore her hair up.

Samantha was well aware that she could probably cut a more striking appearance if she let her long, wavy brown hair flow out over her shoulders, if she replaced her light natural make-up with a more dramatic look, then dolled herself up in figure-hugging feminine frippery, rather than the tailored suits and blouses she chose to wear. Even when going out at night she didn't wear sexy evening gear, opting for trousers—usually black—and silk shirts in neutral colours. But she was comfortable the way she was, and felt foolish and self-conscious whenever she tried a different look.

A sardonic smile crossed her lips as she tried to picture how Guy would react if she came into the office wearing a flashily styled, brightly coloured dress.

Her heart turned over at the thought that he might not notice a single thing.

The sound of a door opening and shutting made her jump. Surely it couldn't be Guy this early?

She hurried from the wash-room and gawped at the sight of her boss leaning against the kitchenette doorway and looking not at all well. Shocked eyes ran over his dishevelled appearance. He hadn't shaved; no comb had touched his hair. And his charcoal-grey suit looked as if he'd slept in it.

'My God, Guy, what's happened to you?' she blurted out.

CHAPTER TWO

GUY remained grimly silent, levering himself away from the door-jamb and scooping a packet of cigarettes out of his jacket pocket. Samantha stared in amazement. Surely he wasn't going to smoke, was he? He certainly wouldn't if his date with sexy Debra had reached its logical conclusion. In bed.

Samantha watched with heartbeat suspended as he extracted the last cigarette from the gold box and shoved it in his mouth. He tossed the empty container in the direction of the waste-paper basket in the corner. It fell in, a perfect goal.

Her heart started thudding as he fished his lighter out of his trouser pocket, flicked it to flame and lit the cigarette, snapping the lighter shut afterwards and drawing in deeply.

Her relief was so gut-wrenching that she felt like crying. Oh, God! What had she come to with this man?

'Dad's in hospital,' he said abruptly. 'Heart attack. He's in Intensive Care.'

Samantha's heart twisted with dismay and guilt. There she'd been, consumed with Guy's sex life, and he had spent the night worrying at his father's possible deathbed.

'Oh, how awful for you,' she cried. She knew how close he and his father were. Mr Haywood senior was always popping in to the office for a chat with his son, and Guy often went fishing with him at weekends. He would be devastated if his dad died. He *already* looked devastated.

Samantha wanted to hug him, hold him, comfort him. But how could she? All she could do was try to say the right things. 'I hope he'll be all right,' she added gently. 'What hospital is he in?'

'St Vincent's.'

'Well, that's the best place he could be,' she soothed. 'What do the doctors say? What are his chances?'

Guy heaved a weary sigh. Smoke curled around his head. 'They're reservedly hopeful. Apparently if you survive the first few hours after the initial attack you have a good chance of a complete recovery. At least, that's the theory,' he added with a caustic edge to his voice. 'He looks like death warmed up.'

'You don't look much better.' Samantha walked over to the small kitchen counter next to the sink and turned off the boiling kettle. 'Let me get you some coffee.'

He flashed her a grateful glance. 'Thanks. It's been a long night. It was after midnight when the call came from the hospital. Debra and I had just got back to my place after the show. We raced straight to the hospital. I've been there ever since. The doctor finally insisted I go home, but I didn't want to go back to an empty house.'

'Empty?' She looked up from where she was spooning instant coffee into two brown stoneware mugs. 'Why is it empty?'

A couple of years ago Guy had sold his terraced house in Paddington and bought a harbour-side mansion, more suited to entertaining on a large scale. At the same time he had hired a childless couple to live in to be cook-housekeeper and handyman-gardener. In their fifties, Leon and Barbara Parker were devoted to both their generous employer and his beautiful home. 'Where are Barbara and Leon?'

'Gone interstate for a nephew's wedding.' A scowl crossed his handsomely ravaged face. 'The bane of the human race, weddings! Look what happened to this office when you went to one. Not only do they put people out by having to go to them, but in a couple of years it's all down the drain anyway when the besotted fools become *unbesotted* and get divorced!'

Samantha shook her head. She could never agree with Guy's cynical attitude to marriage. The divorce rate in Australia wasn't that bad. OK, so his father had married and divorced three times over the past twenty-five years, but his first marriage—to Guy's mother—had not ended that way. Guy had told her that the first Mrs Haywood had died of kidney failure when he was ten years old.

'Not all marriages end in divorce,' she pointed out sensibly. 'And not all people marry just for sex.'

'Most men do,' he scorned. 'And what happens? Six to eighteen months later the passion dies, and so does the marriage. If they stay together longer than that it's probably only for the sake of the children. Believe me, I know.'

It crossed her mind that his father and mother might not have been too happy in their marriage. Not that she thought this an excuse for Guy's cynicism. Nor for the callous way he treated the women in his life. Two wrongs did not make a right, she always believed. But it did make her understand him better.

'*Some* men might marry just for sex,' she argued calmly. 'But some men don't. Look, this is hardly the time for a deep and meaningful discussion on marriage. You're dead on your feet. Why don't you have a nap on the chesterfield in your office?' she suggested as she added the boiling water to the coffee. 'I've a pillow and blanket in the bottom of the old filing cabinet here.'

His laugh was dry. 'What *don't* you have in the bottom of that thing?'

'Never you mind,' she chided. 'It's my personal emergency store.'

'Well, this is certainly an emergency.' He scooped up his coffee, which he took black and unsweetened, and turned to leave. 'Drag them out and bring them in in ten minutes, will you? I've got a few phone calls to make first.'

He began to walk away, then turned and gave her a look that was dangerously close to admiration. Samantha felt it jolt her all the way down to her toes.

'I'll bet the smell of hospitals doesn't make *you* feel like fainting,' he said.

She frowned. 'No. Why?'

'Darling Debra couldn't stay with me at St Vincent's for more than five minutes. Said she was going to pass out.' His tone was definitely derisive. 'Truly, Sam, some women are really pathetic when it comes to the realities of life. Thank God my secretary isn't one of them!'

He smiled at her then, an exhausted but wickedly sexy smile. 'Though she could do with some straightening out on the motives of the male race. Perhaps when I feel more on top of things I'll give you the benefit of my wisdom and experience and save you future heartache. Tell you all you should know about us bad boys.'

Suddenly a black cloud passed over his face. 'Oh, I forgot. You're leaving...'

She swallowed. 'Not for two months.' Did her voice sound funny to him? It did to her. God, why did he have to smile at her like that, and why did it have to reduce her insides to jelly?

His eyes narrowed in black puzzlement. 'I thought you'd change your mind, you know. I was sure you would.'

'My resignation stands,' she reaffirmed, a little too fiercely.

His face turned stubborn, his strong jaw squaring. 'We'll see about that, Samantha Peters. We'll see!' And he stalked off into his own office, leaving her feeling both annoyed and unnerved.

If he thinks he can talk me out of leaving he's sorely mistaken, she thought irritably. He doesn't really care about me personally. All he cares about is having his own way, having his damned ship run like clockwork.

It worried her momentarily that on the whole he tended to get his way in most things.

Well, not this time, she decided. Definitely not!

Ten minutes later she steeled her agitated nerves and took the pillow and blanket in, finding Guy still on the phone.

'Yes, I'm sorry too, Debra,' he was saying in a distinctly bored voice.

Samantha's spirits soared, despite everything. Clearly dear Debra's desertion in the line of fire last night had not been a big hit. Once a person blotted their copybook with Guy, that was usually the end of them. A typical Scorpio, he was not at his best when it came to forgiving and forgetting.

'No, I can't see any night of mine free for quite a while,' he said brusquely. 'I'll be visiting Dad in the hospital each evening and I've got a hitch or two at work...' This with a baleful glare at Samantha. She returned it with a sanguine smile.

'What was that? Oh...well, the doctor was quite pleased with him when I rang just now. He's conscious and they're going to do some test or other on him this morning to see what the main trouble is... Yes, I'll give you a call some time. As far as that other matter is concerned, I don't think there's any point in your changing managers at this stage. Alex is looking after you quite well from what I can see and, to be frank, I'm not taking any more clients at the moment... Yes, you do that. Bye.'

By the time the receiver was placed in its cradle Samantha could see that Debra had already been forgotten. *C'est la vie*, she thought, not without a certain malicious pleasure. She herself might be making an exit from Guy's life but it didn't stop her feeling female satisfaction over another woman's failure.

The object of all these thoughts reached for another cigarette and lit up. There were already several butts in the ashtray beside him, and Samantha felt compelled to speak up.

'Your father was a smoker,' she warned carefully. 'I'm sure you already know smoking is one of the major factors contributing to heart trouble.'

He leant back in the chair and dragged deeply. Icy blue eyes lanced her face. 'The one thing I don't need from women,' he said coldly, 'is mothering.'

Another day she would have ignored his rudeness. But not today. 'Good,' she retorted, and dumped the pillow and blanket on the leather sofa. 'Make up your own bed, then!'

She was about to add that in future he could make his own damned coffee too, but, in truth, he often made his own, never having been one of those bosses who got his secretary to do personal tasks. He looked after himself very well.

'For pity's sake, Sam, don't go getting touchy on me,' he snapped, jerking forward in the chair. 'I'm not in the mood.' But he did stub out the cigarette. 'Besides, why should you care what I do? In sixty days you won't have to watch me commit slow suicide any more.'

He rose from behind the desk and began walking around towards where she was standing near the sofa. It crossed her mind that he had no right to look so disgustingly attractive when he was such a mess.

'You know what, Sam?' he said as he drew near. 'I don't think you'll go through with it in the end. I don't think you'll be able to actually leave when it comes to the crunch.'

'Really?' She folded her arms in a defensive gesture. 'And what makes you think that?' For all her outward composure, inside she felt rattled. There was still a small part of her that agreed with him.

'Because, my dear Sam...' he stopped barely an arm's length from her, giving her the full blast of his most confident face '...I saw the way you looked when we were going through the files yesterday, and later, when we were discussing plans for that tour. This job is the staff of your life. It's your bread and butter. Your soul. Now don't deny it. You've been with me since shortly after the start. You're as much an integral part of Haywood Promotions as I am. We're a team, you and I. An inseparable team!'

Those beautiful blue eyes bored into hers and she wanted to run as fast as she could, away from his intuition, away from his knowledge, away from *him*!

'What would you say,' he asked in his most persuasive voice, 'if I offered you something very different from being just my secretary?'

Her heart jumped into her throat and stopped there. Good God! Surely he couldn't possibly mean what she hoped he meant?

'Such as what?' she managed to get out.

'Such as a minor partnership, a share in the company.'

Samantha's heart dropped back into place. Oh, what an idiot she was to even dream for a minute that he could mean anything else. Where were her brains?

I'll tell you where, a cruel voice lambasted. In your stupid damned female hormones, that's where! Once this man gets within three feet of you, off goes your head and on goes a pumpkin!

'I...' She cleared her throat and tried again. 'I'd still have to say no.'

'*Have* to?' he repeated, taken aback. He stared at her for several seconds, but she volunteered no further information. Finally he shook his head in exasperation. 'Something's going on here that I don't quite understand.'

Making a disgruntled sound, he turned away and stripped off his crumpled jacket, throwing it over the back of a chair. The tie followed. In seconds the buttons were released on his cuffs and he was starting to flip open the ones on his shirt front.

Samantha was glued to the spot, her heartbeat taking up the tango as more and more bare male chest was revealed. First there was just a V of tanned flesh, but then there was a sprinkling of dark curly hair and the light and shade of various muscles, honed to perfection by the many hours he spent in the gym. As the last button gave way she forced herself to turn and walk towards the door.

'But never you fear,' he called after her. 'I'll work it out. In the end I'll know just why you're leaving me. And it's got nothing to do with needing a break or... Good *God*!'

She spun round at his shocked tone, only to find herself staring not at his startled expression, but at his completely naked torso. Desperately she lifted her eyes up to his, but the damage had been done, and her peripheral vision was still taking in far too much taut male flesh.

She was panic-stricken at the directions her mind kept taking. Surely her thoughts and feelings must be showing in her face, her eyes?

'You're not *pregnant*, are you?' he accused.

She was wildly tempted to laugh in his face. Instead she put her energies into trying to get a hold of her thoughts. The exercise was not entirely successful.

'No, Guy,' she said stiffly. 'I'm not pregnant.'

He looked relieved, then annoyed with himself. 'No. Stupid of me. You wouldn't be. Not you. Sorry.' He yawned, spreading out the blanket with a flick of his wrists. 'I guess I'm not thinking straight this morning. I'll talk to you about it again tomorrow, make you see reason.'

'Tomorrow's Saturday,' she pointed out curtly.

'Oh... so it is.' He crawled in under the blanket and laid down his head with a sigh. 'Monday, then. Wake me around two, will you, Sam, like a good girl?'

She woke him at one because a call had come through from the hospital that his father's tests had shown massive blockages of the arteries. The doctor needed immediate permission for a triple bypass. Without it, the chance of a second fatal attack was inevitable and imminent.

Samantha offered to accompany Guy to the hospital but he insisted she stay and hold the fort at the office. In truth, she was glad about this decision, for it gave her the opportunity to regather her defences where he was concerned.

Truly, she was getting worse! Never before had her love for him deteriorated into being so openly lustful. Of course, she had fantasised making love to him, but in the privacy of her night-time dreams, not here in the office. Neither had her fantasies been so blatantly sexual before. They'd always been loving and romantic, sweet and tender.

There'd been nothing sweet and tender in what she had wanted this morning on sighting Guy's bare chest. Her desires had been very basic, to say the least. And they hadn't completely receded either. The encounter had left her feeling physically restless, definitely agitated, decidedly angry.

She had been up and down ever since Guy had left the office, walking around, making coffee, staring out of windows, watching the rain.

This was sexual arousal such as she had never felt before, she admitted in the end. The sort of sexual arousal one read about but never envisaged feeling oneself. Intense...compelling...oddly without conscience.

It kept urging her not to run away from her job and her feelings, not to take any notice of things like pride and self-respect. You want this man, a wicked little voice whispered in her ear. If you can't win his love then settle for his lovemaking. And you haven't got a hope in Hades of getting even *that* if you leave. He'll forget you as quickly as he forgot Debra. If you want something in this world, girl, you have to go after it!

For a few seconds she felt high on a surge of positive thinking, but she was quickly dumped down, swamped by reality, rather than daydreams. How could she successfully seduce a man who had never shown any signs of being sexually attracted to her? It seemed an impossible problem.

She sat back down at her desk and thought and thought.

So what if he's never thought of you in that way before? she finally resolved. You're a reasonably attractive woman, aren't you? He's a highly sexed man, with needs that aren't being met at this moment. You could meet them, couldn't you? All you have to do is convince him how convenient it would be for you to be his mistress. Good heavens, men are doing it all the time, sleeping with their secretaries. And love rarely comes into it on their side. It was mostly nothing more than a sexual convenience, from what she had seen and heard.

The word 'convenience' stuck out like a sore thumb in Samantha's mind. That was the hook which would appeal to Guy most of all.

It came to her quite abruptly, the daring proposition.

What, she thought, wide-eyed and heart thudding, would Guy say if I offered to stay on as his secretary, provided he became my lover?

She could see it now. He would be initially surprised, then thoughtful. Finally he would look up and say, 'Good idea, Sam.'

The phone rang, making her jump as though she had been found with her hand in the biscuit tin. A guilty conscience, she recognised, and snatched up the receiver.

'Haywood Promotions.'

'It's me, Sam.'

She swallowed. Guy... His voice brought home to her that her boss was a flesh and blood man, not a fantasy person who could be made to react as one wanted. This man was one of the most handsome, intelligent, successful, dynamic men in Australia, who could snap his fingers and have just about any woman he wanted. He was not about to be manipulated into an affair by a silly secretary. If she made her ridiculous proposition he would look at her as if she was mad. And probably laugh.

If, by the remotest possibility, he took the proposal seriously he would want to know why. Girls these days could get sex wherever they wanted it. They didn't have to blackmail their bosses for it.

It wouldn't take him long to figure out she'd fallen in love with him and, by golly, her exit would come pretty fast after that. Guy Haywood was not in the business of keeping love-struck women in his office, or in his life. She suspected there had been a few ladies in the past who had fancied him as more than a lover and that they had been given short shrift indeed.

The daring proposition went out of the window.

Which was just as well, she thought wretchedly. She wouldn't have had the guts to do it, anyway.

'Yes,' she said flatly. 'What do you want?'

'You sound terrible. Look, Sam, you have to tell me what's going on with you. It's bothering me and I can't wait till Monday. Is it anything I've done? For pity's sake, tell me if it is.'

It's something you haven't done, she thought miserably. Why can't you be a normal boss and make a pass at your secretary? Why can't you take me out to dinner and then to a motel? I won't mind. Really I won't.

'It's nothing you've done,' she told him. 'You've been a perfect gentleman to work for.' Unfortunately...

'Then what is it, dammit?'

'It's exactly as I said, Guy. I want to change the direction of my life. And I want to get out of Sydney.'

'Aah... Now I get it. It's a man, isn't it?'

She hesitated, then decided the truth would do quite well. 'Yes, Guy. You're right. It's a man.'

'What's the problem?' he probed. 'Is it that he wants you and you don't want him, or the other way around.'

It perversely amused her that he didn't use the word 'love'. It just wasn't in his dictionary when it came to man-woman relationships. 'The other way around,' she admitted.

Guy digested that for a few seconds. 'I see... You never talk about your personal life to me, do you? I just realised I don't know much about you in that regard. Have you been having a... relationship with this man, a...close relationship?'

She smiled wryly to herself. For all Guy's wordliness, he couldn't seem to come out with the bare facts in front of her. Truly, did he think that at twenty-five she was a total innocent? Why not ask her straight out if she was sleeping with the man? Still, it gave her the opportunity to mislead him without actually lying. 'Oh, yes,' she said. 'Very close.'

'Goddammit, Sam, you haven't been having an affair with a married man, have you?'

She was taken aback by his shocked, even judgemental tone. That was certainly the kettle calling

the pot black. Though to be honest she had never
known him to have an affair with a married woman.

'No, Guy,' she denied firmly. 'He's not married.
And never likely to be.'

'Aah, so that's it. The blighter won't marry you.'

'Not in a million years!'

'That's no reason to quit Sydney and a perfectly
good job.'

'I think it is.'

'I aim to talk you out of going.'

'You can try. Meanwhile I'll ring the head-hunters
and line some interviews up for you.'

'Don't bother,' he snarled.

'Guy...' There was no mistaking her exasperated tone.

'If I have to I'll take Mrs Walton,' he said with
a sigh. 'At least I know her. The last thing I want
is one of those ambitious, vampirish secretaries who
try to run the show, their boss included.'

'She'll be thrilled,' Samantha said. 'I'll ring her
right away.'

'You do that.' He let out another sigh. 'God,
Sam, hospitals are depressing places.'

'How *is* your father?' she asked with genuine
concern. She didn't know Martin Haywood very
well, but what she had seen she couldn't help liking.
He was a charming rogue, just like his son.

'Not good. The triple bypass is scheduled for
tomorrow morning, most unusual for a Saturday,
it seems. They only have theatre during the weekend
if it's a life and death matter, so I'm not getting
my hopes up.'

'He'll have the best of care,' she reassured.

'Maybe so. But I feel very pessimistic about it
all.'

'He's not old, though. What is he? Late fifties?'

'Fifty-seven. But he's abused himself over the years. No proper exercise. Wine...women...'

Samantha thought it best not to add anything about the smoking at this moment, knowing Guy himself was probably puffing away like mad at the other end of the line. He always did when he was tense or worried about something.

'I've only just realised I might have to face his dying and, damn it all, Sam, I don't like it. I don't like it one bit!'

He sounded terribly distressed, which made Samantha feel guilty. She'd picked a rotten time to resign on him, but it had to be done, even more so after what had happened earlier today. Out of sight was out of mind, she hoped. And if it was cowardly of her to run away then she was a coward! There was no viable alternative. If there were she would take it.

'I wish there were something I could do to help,' she murmured truthfully.

Any normal secretary could have offered to cook him a meal, since his housekeeper was away, but she didn't dare. Her feelings towards Guy had tipped over a dangerous edge today and it worried her that she wouldn't always be able to control them. Best she keep well away from him in any social sense. It would be hard enough dampening down these newly wayward desires at work without inviting disaster elsewhere.

'There's nothing you can do for me,' Guy stated, 'except stay on as my secretary.'

'Please, Guy, drop it.'

'All right,' he sighed. 'I'll drop it. For now... See you Monday morning, Sam.'

He hung up.

Monday morning, she mused, replacing the dead receiver. That was three days away. In three days she should have herself firmly under control again.

CHAPTER THREE

As FATE would have it, Samantha was not to see Guy the following Monday. Or the Tuesday for that matter. His father's operation had been a technical success, but his recovery less so. He remained in Intensive Care in a coma, with Guy hardly leaving the hospital except to ring the office.

'You'd think one of those precious ex-wives of his would have shown up to see how he's faring, wouldn't you?' he growled during his second call for Tuesday. It was four-fifteen in the afternoon. 'I let each one of them know about the operation and they all mouthed meaningless wishes for Dad's welfare, but not an appearance between the three of them.'

'You sound tired, Guy,' Samantha said gently. 'Why don't you go home and have a proper night's sleep?'

'Can't.'

'Why ever not?'

'Dad needs me.'

'But he's unconscious,' she pointed out. 'You can't really do anything.'

'Yes, I can. I can talk to him, let him know it's important to someone for him to pull through. I've read where coma patients can hear more than people realise.'

'Yes . . . I've read that too.' Samantha thought it wonderful for a grown man to love his father so much, and would have dearly liked to be by Guy's side at the hospital, helping him in a more personal way during this time of trial. But a secretary could hardly presume to take such an intimate role and she supposed she *was* helping by looking after his business in ~~his~~ absence.

'I've lined up the bookings for the tour,' she said, knowing that talking about work would distract him from his worry for a little while.

'Already?'

'Mrs Walton helped me. She came in for a few hours yesterday and today. Of course, I couldn't get the Entertainment Centre for Sydney. That's booked out solid for a year. It'll have to be the racecourse. Open-air stuff. Risky, I know. We'll have to insure against rain. Oh, and the *Midday Show* want Frankie for a regular spot. His guest appearance last week was a big hit.'

Frankie Myers was the only comedian Guy handled. Mostly he concentrated on rock singers, musicians and bands. But Frankie was a special case. A Vietnam veteran, he'd initially made a modest living doing a stand-up comedy routine in hotels and clubs. But a growing drinking problem had shown him to be an unreliable gig and, in the end, no one would hire him. He'd been on skid row when Guy had literally tripped over him one night eighteen months ago in the gutter near his home. He'd recognised him, taken him inside, cleaned him up, dried him out and told him he'd make him a success if he gave up drinking for good.

Frankie did just that, and Guy had kept his side of the bargain, helping him update and polish his material and finding him work. But to get a regular spot on the top daytime programme on Australian television would mean unlimited exposure and a guarantee of success.

'That's terrific,' Guy said, his voice smiling. 'He deserves a break, the poor bastard.'

'He'd never have done it without your encouragement and help.'

'True.' Modesty was not one of Guy's virtucs. 'Anything else to report?'

'No. Nothing I can't handle.'

'I don't know when I'll be in...'

'Don't worry. Mrs Walton and I will keep the home fires burning.'

'You're a girl in a million, Sam. See you.'

Samantha's heart turned over as she heard the line go dead. Oh, Guy... You like me. I know you do. And liking can turn to love, given the chance.

Darn it all, she thought with a surge of irritation. Why couldn't I have been born tiny and blonde?

When the phone rang again twenty minutes later she was about to pack and go home. She looked at the phone with a measure of distaste. She seemed to have spent the whole day on the thing and had had enough.

'Hayward Promotions?' she said somewhat impatiently as she snatched it up.

'It's your boss again. Guess what? Dad's conscious. Sam, I think he's going to make it!'

She let out a shuddering sigh of relief. 'That's wonderful, Guy. I'm so happy for you.'

'I'll be in first thing in the morning. Well...not quite first thing. Around elevenish. I have some sleep to catch up on.'

He was gone before she could say another word, leaving her with a ridiculous grin on her face. Guy's happiness would always be her happiness.

What would there be, she worried later as she stepped outside into a still soggy Sydney, to make her happy when she didn't see him any more?

There seemed to be no answer for her.

The office got back to relative normality after that—if battling to block out one's dangerously escalating desire for one's boss could be considered normal.

Guy's father made rapid improvement. In fact he was discharged from hospital and sent home within two weeks of his becoming conscious, refusing to go to Guy's place, hiring a private nurse and housekeeper to look after him in his own penthouse apartment. Martin Haywood was not short of a dollar, having made a fortune as an inventor of an engineering process that had revolutionised high-rise building methods.

But, despite his father's recovery, Samantha could sense something troubling Guy. If he'd regularly tried to persuade her not to leave she might have thought *she* was the problem, but he seemed to have almost forgotten that soon she'd be gone. Many a time she would go into his office to find him standing at the window across the room, staring blankly out over the building tops. Then when she spoke to him he would turn round, and it would be several seconds before he'd even focus on her.

Not only that, he seemed to have lost all interest in his business, actually cutting down on the people he looked after, calling them and telling them to find another manager. She began to worry that he might not be feeling well himself, but hesitated to ask. He hated that kind of fussing. Besides, she rather fancied it was an emotional problem, not a physical one.

Unless, of course, it was sex, she decided one afternoon when he was particularly distracted. Or the lack of it. He was smoking more than ever, which meant there was no new blonde in his life.

Samantha would have known if there were, anyway. All of Guy's girlfriends were always so besotted with him that they couldn't leave him alone. There would be phone calls and drop-in visits; luncheon dates; little presents delivered. Odd, that, she always thought. His women liked to give him things, not the other way around. She'd never known Guy to send flowers to a woman in his life.

No, clearly there wasn't any new dolly-bird helping him make it through the night.

She herself wasn't sleeping too well either.

Samantha was to find out exactly what was eating at him one Thursday in May, four weeks to the day after she had handed in her resignation. Mrs Walton had gone home after her weekly four hours of apprenticeship, and Samantha was catching up on some correspondence, mostly written confirmation of bookings.

'Fancy some coffee?' Guy asked as he wandered out of his office towards her desk.

'Yes, thanks,' she answered, looking up. Then wished she hadn't. She'd forgotten how gorgeous he looked that day, in a navy suit and pale blue shirt. Blue was definitely his colour, seemingly highlighting his striking blue eyes.

Her gaze followed him as he moved past her desk and into the kitchen. It struck her that she had never seen him dressed in anything but a suit, which was surprisingly conventional in this day and age, particularly with someone of Guy's background.

He'd been a rocker in his younger days, a drummer in a band. Much to his father's disgust at the time. Apparently Guy had formed the band while doing an engineering degree at university, having so much success with it that the degree had never been finished. When the band had finally broken up a decade later he'd directed his talents and natural intelligence into the managerial side of showbiz, thereby regaining parental approval.

Samantha wondered if his conventional dressing was his way of impressing on his business contacts that his wild old rocker days were a thing of the past. Whatever the reason, he always looked great to Samantha.

Guy wandered back in with the two coffees, placed hers carefully beside her computer, then perched on the far corner of her desk while he sipped his.

'Thanks again,' she said, feeling not a hint of premonition. Making her coffee and stopping for a brief chat was something Guy did quite often. The only feeling Samantha was enduring was the hot prickle of sexual awareness that plagued her now whenever he was so physically close. One more month, she thought ruefully as she sipped the coffee, and this type of torture would be over.

'You know what, Sam?' he sighed. 'Life's a bitch.'

'Oh?' She was startled by this remark. It was not like Guy to be negative or pessimistic in anything. Most of the time he exuded a confidence bordering on arrogance. But then, he hadn't been himself lately, had he? Not since his father's heart trouble. 'Why do you say that?' she asked.

He left his coffee and slid off the end of the desk, strolling across to stand in his now familiar pose at the nearest window, his back to her. 'I have this problem,' he said in a low, almost reluctant voice. 'A damned impossible problem.'

He turned then and walked back towards her with a self-mocking expression on his face. 'God knows why I'm telling you. You can't help me. No one can really. I can see it's a crazy problem, totally illogical, with no workable solution. The trouble is I can't put it out of my mind.' He stood in front of her desk, picked up his coffee and drank deeply.

'Why don't you just tell me what this crazy, illogical and unworkable problem is?' she suggested. 'At least you'll have it off your chest then. Don't you think I've noticed something's been bothering you?'

He frowned at her. 'You didn't say anything.'

She shrugged. 'I thought it might be because of my leaving.' Or something else she couldn't exactly mention, like sexual frustration.

He rubbed his forehead with an agitated finger. 'No...that's not it. If you're going to go then you're going to go. I hate the idea, but I'm not going to beat my head up against a brick wall, and I can see when you make up your mind about something, Samantha Peters, you're a brick wall.'

She wasn't sure whether that was a compliment or not. 'Then what is it?' she persisted.

He swallowed the final slurp of coffee, then exhaled a ragged breath. 'You'll think I'm off my tree, but the simple truth is . . . I want a child.'

Samantha was very grateful that she was sitting down. And that she didn't have the hot coffee to her mouth. As it was she almost dropped the damned mug. Just in time she tightened her fingers, then lowered it carefully to the desk-top. 'You want a child,' she repeated, trying not to look as stunned as she felt.

'Yes,' he said. 'A child. A son or a daughter. When Dad nearly died I realised how God awful empty my life would be without him. Yet I *will* be without him one day. After he's gone there'll be no one in this world who cares if I live or die. Not for the right reason, anyway.'

He was looking right at her and she was sure he would have to see how her eyes started shining, see the burning love she carried in her heart for him written all over her face.

Apparently, he didn't, his unseeing gaze turned inward on to his own troubled soul. 'I know it's a mad idea,' he said impatiently. 'You don't have to tell me how mad! But still . . .' His eyes took on that far-away look, as though he was imagining what it would be like to be a father and was entranced by the idea.

Surreptitiously Samantha put the phone on hold. She didn't want a single thing interrupting *this* conversation.

His eyes snapped back to the present and he glared at her. 'Do you think I'm mad?' he demanded.

'Not at all,' she said as composedly as she could manage. 'It's a basic human drive to reproduce. Perfectly normal.'

Surprise lit his face. 'Yes, yes, it is, isn't it?' he enthused, clearly excited by her words. 'As basic as food, and sex.' He laughed. 'Well, of course that was the original idea behind sex, wasn't it? Reproducing. It took human ingenuity to separate the two.'

Samantha swallowed. She wasn't sure where all this was leading, but she was on the edge of her seat with breathless anticipation.

Guy paced back over to the window, and stood there, astride and arrogant, for a few seconds. But then he whirled to face her, his expression frustrated. 'But surely you can see my problem? You know what I'm like, Sam. Marriage is not for me and never will be. I wasn't meant to sleep with the same woman for the rest of my life. Hell, I'm hard pushed to make it to six months before I'm bored out of my mind. I won't marry a woman just to have a child when I know it will end in divorce.'

Samantha accepted this quite easily. It was the pattern of his life so far. If only he could see that sex without love *had* to be boring in the end. Not that she said as much. She was too enthralled in hearing what he was going to come out with next.

'The same goes for these so-called *love-children*,' he went on with a derisive wave of his hand. 'What happens when the parents fall out of love? Just as devastating a situation for the child as divorce. Besides,' he added scathingly, 'I've never been in love in my life and, quite frankly, I'm thankful I haven't. Makes idiots of the most sensible sane men!'

And women, Samantha added to herself with a silent groan.

'No,' he pronounced. 'I discarded both of those ideas weeks ago, which left me with two remaining possible courses of action,' he stated, walking slowly back to her desk. 'Firstly, I thought of paying a surrogate mother to have the child by artificial insemination and hand it over after it was born. But that's awfully risky. She could change her mind and take me to court later and get the child back. I would never let a child of mine be an emotional football!'

The vehemence behind these last words gave Samantha another glimpse of a man harbouring a lot of pain. Since Guy loved his father without reservation, she could only imagine that his mother had to be the responsible one.

'Not only that,' he growled, 'but I find the concept of artificial insemination distasteful. Maybe I'm a closet romantic, but I prefer to conceive my child the normal way, not with me as a mere extension of a test-tube. If I'm going to embrace the most important commitment a man can make—that of fatherhood—I want to be involved in a personal way right from the start. Damn it, I *need* to be involved. It'll be *my child*!'

Samantha could only stare at Guy, so astounded was she to even hear the word 'commitment' come out of his mouth, let alone in such a passionate and caring way. It came to her quite forcibly that any future child of his would be a very lucky boy or girl indeed. For Guy would undoubtedly love it with all the love he'd never before bestowed on another human being, except perhaps his own father.

For a moment her mind drifted to the most impossible fantasy—of this unexpectedly emotional Guy somehow finding out he'd loved her all along, of his proposing marriage, of their having this much longed-for child together. She suppressed a sigh and gave her full attention back to her darkly frowning boss.

'Which brings me to the second, final and ultimate solution to my problem,' Guy went on, a dry sarcasm creeping into his voice. 'I find some nice single co-operative lady who wants to have my child, will agree to let me share its upbringing, but who won't make any demands on me other than financial ones. Now isn't that the best fairy-story of a female you ever heard?' He threw his hands up in the air in exasperated defeat. 'Find me such a woman, Sam, and I'll give you every cent I have!'

Samantha's heart went into total seizure.

Not so her mind!

My God, it virtually exploded. Did you hear what he just said, what he wants? This is your chance, your wildest dream come true.

Well, not quite, harsh reality answered. He's not offering love and marriage. But he is offering his body and his *child*! A life-long bond that would tie him to you forever!

That's more than you ever hoped for. More than your other proposition would have given you. Much more. For this leaves you with your pride and self-respect.

All you have to do is dare...

But to succeed with such a daring proposition she would have to be very calm. Super-calm. One whiff of emotional involvement and Guy would cut her dead.

'This nice single co-operative lady,' she drawled, her heart pounding so loudly in her chest that she was certain he must hear it, 'would she have to be a blonde?'

Penetrating blue eyes locked on to hers and a slow sardonic smile creased his mouth. 'You've got me taped, haven't you, Sam? But I think that would be asking for a little too much, wouldn't you?' He made a scornful sound. 'This saint-like creature fitting my physical preference as well?'

'In that case...what about me?' she said, amazing herself with her ultra-casual tone. 'Would I do?'

There was no doubt she had stunned him. For a good few seconds he simply stared at her, and then he fulfilled her worst nightmare. He laughed.

Her face must have shown something, for suddenly he stopped and frowned at her. 'My God, you mean it, don't you?'

She recovered, to give a nonchalant shrug. 'Of course. I never say what I don't mean. Apparently *you* do, though. Otherwise you wouldn't find my offer so amusing. You'd be thanking your lucky stars that you've found a woman prepared to go along with your—er—highly unusual suggestion.'

Again he stared at her, as one did at a person who had done something alien to what you would always have imagined them capable of. 'But why on earth would you be prepared to do such a thing?' he demanded to know. 'It doesn't make sense. What's in it for *you*?'

She wanted to close her eyes but she couldn't. She wanted to get up and run away. But this was her chance, the only one she would ever get and, by golly, she was going to grab it with both hands!

'I've always wanted children,' she said truthfully. 'Since the man I love doesn't love me back and will never marry me, my chances of having a child look slim. I'll never marry anyone else. That I know.'

'What rubbish!' Guy derided. 'You're a young woman. You'll fall in love again.'

'No, I won't,' she argued levelly. 'I'm a brick wall, remember. I won't fall in love again. At least, not for a long, long time. And I'm not that young. I'm twenty-five, Guy, going on twenty-six. If I'm going to have a child I would like to have one soon. I have to admit I would never have thought of this myself and I would never have dared do it in a small country town. But here...in the city...it's different.'

He was literally gaping at her.

'Yes, I do realise I've surprised you,' she went on coolly. 'To tell the truth, I'm rather surprised myself. But if you think about it it's the perfect solution for both of us. We already like each other, respect each other. We're friends. And I do appreciate what sort of man you are. I understand that after I've conceived you would wish to return to your former free and easy lifestyle. Of course, I would have to ask that there would be no other women till then...'

The blue eyes had continued to widen with shock during her speech. But Samantha was convinced that this was the manner to adopt. If she deviated from her coolly competent self Guy might smell a rat.

She almost laughed at the irony of this thought. *He* was the rat, wasn't he? Not herself. Oh, lord, what in heaven's name was she doing?

You're going after what you want, her love-filled heart urged. Let this opportunity go by and you'll regret it for the rest of your life.

Stiffening her spine, she shoved any doubts aside and plunged on. 'Naturally, as you've already indicated, I would expect you to look after my future in a financial sense, perhaps with that partnership you offered me a few weeks ago. If that was the case I would be prepared to stay on here, at least till the baby was born. After that—who knows? Best to take these things one step at a time, don't you think?'

She set steady hazel eyes on him. 'Well, Guy? What do you say? Good idea or bad idea?' Inside, every part of her was trembling with nervous anticipation. She recognised that such an arrangement was outrageous, even *scandalous*, but she refused to go back on any of it. Loving Guy as she did—wanting him as she did—made her oblivious to the norms of social convention.

He blinked once. Then twice. Then scratched his head. 'I have to be honest with you, Sam. You've floored me. You've really floored me!'

'I can see that,' she said, not without a trace of dry amusement. 'Would you like a day to think it over? Or a month maybe? You have a month before I leave.'

'Good God, do you have to sound so cool about it? We're not talking about a business merger here, but a rather more personal one. Might I remind you that to have a baby we would have to go to bed together? Not once, or twice. But maybe many times.'

A tremor raced all through her, but she didn't think he noticed. She kept her expression perfectly bland. 'Yes, Guy,' she managed to say quite calmly. 'I do realise that. Being a country girl, having babies holds no mystery for me.'

Reproach flashed into those piercing blue eyes. 'Goddamit, woman,' he grated out, 'we're not two sheep rutting away in a paddock! We're human beings, with feelings and...sensitivity. When I make love to a woman I have to feel like it. I can't just turn it on like a tap. A woman might be able to merely lie there, but a man can't fake it, you know!'

A chill shivered through Samantha. This was the bottom line, wasn't it? The ultimate rejection. 'Do you find me so unattractive, Guy,' she said with barely concealed hurt, 'that making love to me is virtually an impossibility?'

He seemed uncomfortable. Also slightly perplexed. His eyes lanced her face, then travelled downwards over her shoulders and lower. In spite of being well disguised by her suit jacket, her full breasts tingled disconcertingly as his eyes skated over them. But she kept her chin up, boldly, bravely.

He shook his head, dragging in then expelling a ragged breath. He leant on the front of the desk, setting reasoning eyes upon her. 'All I'm saying, Sam, is that I have never looked at you in a sexual fashion. That doesn't mean you're not an attractive woman. Of course you are. I'm not blind. I dare say I *could* take you to bed successfully if I put my mind to it, but——'

'Well, then,' she cut in with icy calm, 'if you want a child the normal way that's exactly what you'll have to do. I doubt you'll find some luscious little blonde who'll fill your other requirements.'

He stared at her for a second, then straightened, his face worried. 'I don't think you've thought this through, Sam. You're acting on the rebound because this other man won't marry you. Believe me, I appreciate your offer and I'd snap it up like *that*...' he clicked his fingers '...if I thought down deep you meant it. You'd make an excellent mother. I couldn't ask for better. But you'd regret it. I know you would. A girl like you should have a proper marriage and a husband who would love you dearly.'

Oh, dear God, she thought brokenly, if he keeps this up I'm going to cry. I know I will!

'I won't regret it,' she rasped. 'It's what I want to do. I'm only sorry you refuse to take me seriously.'

Her thickened tone brought a sharp look.

She swallowed and returned it with what she hoped was a composed face.

She could see the indecision in his, the doubts. He was an intuitive man, and was undoubtedly sensing that there was something here he was missing. 'I'm sorry too, Sam. But I can't get over the feeling that you've rushed into this offer of yours. Look, I... I'll think it over some more to-night,' he agreed reluctantly. 'We'll talk again in the morning.'

Dismay coursed through her. Guy was a black and white person, a man of instant decisions. This 'thinking it over' was his way of letting her down gently. 'All right,' she said flatly.

Guy turned and walked briskly back into the inner office, shutting the door behind him. Samantha stared at the closed door. Slowly, ever so slowly, the tears began to trickle down her face.

CHAPTER FOUR

SAMANTHA was a bundle of nerves the following morning. She was up with the dawn, having slept poorly, then spent a whole hour putting on outfit after outfit, trying to find one that made her look sexy. Of course, nothing did to her eye. She found the exercise so futile and annoying that in the end she put on the first thing that came to hand. A black Chanel-style suit in fine wool, with a black and white striped blouse that tied at the neck. Her hair went up as usual, her make-up nothing to write home about. Perfume she never wore to work.

Breakfast and housework out of the way, Samantha set off, walking briskly to the bus-stop and arriving at the office at eight-thirty—extra-early. A warm autumn sun was shining brightly through the windows as she drew back the curtains, which she took for an omen of doom. How could one expect anything else to go right that day if the weather was gorgeous? When was life that generous?

'You're getting cynical in your old age,' she muttered aloud and went about making herself some strong coffee.

By nine-thirty she was seated at her desk, glancing through the morning paper, her eyes darting to the wall clock every few seconds, then to the door as she awaited Guy's arrival. He wouldn't be late because Rolf Wetherington, his accountant, had an appointment for ten. Samantha wasn't sure how

Guy did it, but he never had to go to other people's offices. They came to him.

He was one of those men who commanded not only respect but personal attention, which he lapped up as his due, resulting in his business associates being even more deferential. In one way this irritated Samantha. Everyone needed bringing down a peg or two occasionally to remind one they were only human. Somehow she couldn't see anyone doing this to Guy. He would remain inviolate in his selfish, egocentric highly planned world.

That was one of the reasons she believed he wouldn't accept her proposal. It was one thing to dream about becoming a father; quite another to put it into action. By now he would have realised that he could hardly jettison the mother of his child from his life as easily as he could one of his girlfriends who had begun to bore him. Being involved with a woman on a level he couldn't totally control would not appeal to Guy at all.

The truth was the surrogate mother option would have suited him admirably—if he'd been able to trust it.

One part of Samantha was semi-relieved that he was going to reject her proposition. Much as she wanted Guy to make love to her, much as she would *adore* to have his child, she had the awful feeling that fantasies come to life often proved disappointing. One always expected too much. Maybe Guy would turn out to be a dreadful father, she pointed out to herself.

Don't be ridiculous, came the scornful reply. Look at him with his own father. They have a *great* relationship. It was the one thing in Guy's life that was steady and strong and secure. Guy would love his child with the same devotion.

Well, maybe he's hopeless in bed, she tried again, desperately looking for reasons not to feel such desolation at his probable rejection.

And maybe the world is flat, was her dry retort.

Come on, girl, you've seen the way his female companions can't keep their hands off him, can't leave him alone for a minute. They're like *leeches*! And what about all those presents they give him, not to mention purring contented looks? Those females are satisfied, darling Samantha. Well and truly.

Not like you, honey-bunch. You don't know the meaning of the word. Fact is, you don't know much about sex at all on a first-hand basis!

Samantha sighed. Other than that fiasco with poor Norman—which was merely a blur in her memory now—her sexual experience was minimal.

Not that she was ignorant about sex. Or in any way physically shy. Once Aunt Vonnie had boosted her looks and her confidence, she'd come to Sydney at age nineteen, a normal healthy teenage girl, quite keen to experience love and romance!

But not as quickly as city boys had wanted her to. They had expected a girl to let them go all the way on the very first date. That just wasn't how she'd been brought up! She hadn't minded kissing and necking, but she had always known she would need to be in love before she could allow total intimacy. It hadn't taken her long to learn that most members of the male sex didn't need to be remotely in love to indulge in anything and everything! They weren't too pleased either when she told them politely, but firmly, that one-night stands and casual sex weren't her scene.

In the end, she had only dated spasmodically and carefully, and waited for her heart to tell her this was it! In the meantime she had changed her job from a boring receptionist-secretary position to Guy's assistant, and for several months had been so caught up in her new job that she'd given up dating altogether.

By the time she had realised she was in love with her boss her circle of male friends had dwindled away to nix. One couldn't expect them to wait around forever.

She had been content for a while to hope and dream, but then those seemingly futile hopes and dreams had begun to get the better of her. One summer, two years after her dreaded discovery, and driven to despair by Guy's latest conquest—a model named Tiffany, of all things!—she had gone on a holiday cruise and quite deliberately set out to have an affair in a desperate attempt to forget Guy.

She'd had no trouble picking up a man—a handsome one too—yet when it had come down to the nitty-gritty she hadn't been able to go through with it. As soon as her hopeful lover had started undressing, all she could think of was that she wanted it to be Guy. In the end she'd burst into tears and run out of the cabin. The next day she hadn't been surprised when her offended admirer had found another girl to spend the rest of the cruise with. Samantha had returned to Sydney and work, more emotionally depressed than ever.

Nevertheless, the experience had brought home to her that she just wasn't made for casual sex. She needed love to make it right for her. Real, deep love. And then she was sure it would be fantastic.

So she had lived on, without men, without sex, going to work and watching her hopes and dreams being crushed time after time.

Today would be the final obliteration...

The phone started ringing.

Samantha glared at it. She didn't want to be talking to someone when Guy came in. She wanted her rejection to be quick. Like an amputation.

Irritated, she snatched up the receiver. 'Haywood Promotions.'

'Hi, Samantha, it's Lisa here.'

She groaned silently. Lisa lived in the same block of units as Samantha—in the flat above, to be precise—and she was the most dreadful chatterbox. In her late twenties and still single, she worked in a public service job in town and would often ring Samantha when bored. But nine thirty-five was a little early to be bored, even for Lisa, so it seemed likely she wanted to ask a favour. Samantha's problem would be getting her off the line afterwards. 'Hi, what can I do for you?'

'How did you know I wanted you to do something for me?' Lisa said in a surprised voice.

Samantha rolled her eyes. 'I didn't, Lisa. It was just a guess. Am I right?'

'Well, yes, you are, actually...'

Samantha's whole body stiffened as the door opened and Guy walked in, looking resplendent in the lightest grey suit and dazzling white shirt. His thick brown hair was slicked back and darkly damp as though he had not long stepped from a shower, which was possible. His home was only a few minutes from the city.

Clear blue eyes caught hers, but he gave nothing away. Seeing her on the phone, he merely nodded and walked briskly on, past her desk and into the kitchenette.

'...So I was hoping you would do that for me. Is that OK?'

Samantha realised with a jolt that she had missed the whole middle of what Lisa had said. 'Er—there was static on the line just now, Lisa. Would you repeat that last bit?'

'I said would you mind taking my washing in from the line after you get home tonight? I'm going to the pub for drinks with some friends straight after work. I tried to catch you this morning but you must have left early.'

'Yes, I did.'

She tried to concentrate on Lisa but one ear was on Guy as he moved around in the small room behind her. What was he thinking? When was he going to tell her? Would he make polite excuses or turn her down flat?

'Oh, by the way,' Lisa raved on, 'you haven't seen Tom lately, have you? I'm worried about him.'

Tom was a huge and homeless ginger cat whom the block of units they both lived in had adopted. He was an old rascal of an animal who wormed his way into everyone's affections with his manipulative personality. When he wanted something—like food and a bed for the night—he would be love on four legs, rubbing and purring and smooching. The next morning he was just as likely to give you the cold shoulder and walk off with his nose in the air.

'That devil,' Samantha laughed, pushing thoughts of Guy to one side as she smiled to herself over Tom's antics. 'I never worry about him. He'll be back when he needs a free meal and a warm body next to him in bed for the night. And, fool that I am, I'll probably let him in and give him what he wants.'

'Yeah...me too. We're all mugs where that cat is concerned.'

'That's true,' Samantha sighed. 'The funny thing is I know he's only conning me. But, once I've let him in and fed him, I just can't seem to resist him. He saunters into my bedroom as if he owns it, and before I know it I'm lifting up the covers and he crawls in with me as if that was where he'd always belonged. Then next morning, after breakfast, he can't wait to leave. Still, that's Tom for you. Take him or leave him, that's his motto.'

'Mmm. Sounds like some men I know,' Lisa said drily.

Samantha slowly became aware of eyes boring into her back. She swung round in her chair to find Guy standing in the doorway to the kitchenette, staring at her as though he'd just found out she was an industrial spy.

'Er—Lisa,' she whispered hurriedly, 'I have to go. I think the boss wants me.'

'I wish he wanted me,' Lisa drawled. 'That man is a hunk. I saw him on TV the other night at the music video awards, and what that man does to a dinner suit is divine!'

'Bye, Lisa.'

'Don't forget the clothes!' she shouted as Samantha hung up.

'Is something wrong?' Samantha said, one hand lifting to self-consciously pat her hair.

His stare became a frustrated glare, his hands coming up to prop on his hips. 'If I hadn't heard it with my own ears I wouldn't have believed it!'

She blinked. 'Believed what?'

He threw up his hands in exasperation. 'Hell, Sam, I thought you were one of the most level-headed females I had ever met. Goddammit, do you know how risky it is to go to bed with a bloke like that Tom you were just talking about on the phone? He sounds like a real bum!'

'Tom?' she repeated in a puzzled tone a split-second before the penny dropped into place.

'Yes, Tom. Surely you can remember him?' Guy's tone was blisteringly sarcastic. 'The one who apparently cons his way into your bed with regular monotony. Tom, the charming devil. Tom, the sodding bastard would be a better description!'

Samantha tried not to laugh as she realised how her conversation with Lisa must have seemed when overheard one-sided. But it was no use. The giggles burst forth.

Guy looked positively appalled. 'This is crazy. Not only do I discover you're leading a dangerously promiscuous private life, but you've got a warped sense of humour as well! And I thought I *knew* you!'

'Tom,' she choked out before he could make any further hysterical accusation, 'is a cat.'

His mouth dropped open, then snapped shut. 'A...*cat*?'

'Yes, a cat.' She grinned at him. 'A vagrant tom who pops into my flat occasionally.'

Guy's mouth took a while to crack a smile, but when it did it did so graciously and apologetically. 'I feel a fool,' he admitted.

'Anyone could have been mistaken,' she excused him, smothering her laughter with difficulty. It hadn't escaped her notice either that once again she had ruffled his feathers. It rather pleased her. Rejected she might be. Taken for granted? Never again!

'No,' he refuted drily. 'I should have known better. After all, you've been with me long enough for me to know you're not that sort of girl at all.'

Every vestige of humour died inside Samantha. He made her sound hopelessly dull and boring. 'And what sort of girl am I?' she quizzed haughtily.

He seemed startled by the question. Or was it her sharply indignant tone?

'Go on, tell me truthfully,' she persisted, piqued to the point of anger. 'I'd like to know. It might explain why you've obviously decided not to take me up on my offer yesterday.' As if that needed saying.

His glance carried surprise before becoming deeply thoughtful. 'The truth, you say?' he mused aloud.

'Oh, definitely the truth.' Her tone was tart. In for a penny, in for a pound, Aunt Vonnie always used to say.

Actually Aunt Vonnie would have liked Guy, she thought desolately as she gazed at his broodingly handsome face. He fulfilled all her aunt's require- ments in a man. Good-looking, well-built, am- bitious, basically honest, but with enough male wickedness to be interesting. The only trouble was he had never developed the ability to fall in love. That, Samantha realised, was a fatal flaw, if ever there was one.

'You're very hard to define, Sam,' he finally said. 'Actually, I've been thinking about you all night and I would say that the quality I admire most in you is your strength of character. Yes, that's it. You have character. And, by the way, you were wrong a moment ago.' He smiled wryly. 'I *have* decided to accept your offer.'

People talked about hearts jumping into people's mouths. Samantha had used to think it was an exaggeration. Now she knew it was true. Hers rocketed upwards, suspended for a second next to her thick tongue before settling back into her chest with a thump.

'But...but...' She scooped in a life-saving breath, her heart hammering in her chest. This wasn't real. This wasn't happening to her. Oh, God, what had she done?

Her flustered reaction brought a frowning look. 'Don't tell me *you've* changed your mind? You vowed you wouldn't.'

'Well...I...' Get a hold of yourself, you idiot! 'No, I haven't,' she said, still shakily.

'You don't sound so sure.'

'It's just that...' She hesitated, unable to find the right words. She couldn't very well say what she was really feeling. That she was totally overwhelmed. Weakly ecstatic. Utterly terrified! 'I was certain you would say no,' she finally managed. 'I guess I'll need some time for it to sink in, to seem...real.'

'It's going to be real all right,' he said drily. 'Very real when it comes to the matter of us going to bed together. But you seemed well able to handle that aspect yesterday. Or is the idea of imminent sex with me too much for you in the cold light of day?' he asked, his eyes never leaving hers.

She gulped. There was no doubt that Guy was watching her closely, observing her reaction. She had the feeling that he was putting her through some sort of test, and she aimed to come through with flying colours.

Arranging her face into a serious expression, she looked him straight in the eye. 'I won't say I don't find the prospect somewhat daunting,' she said. 'But in this case the end justifies the means, wouldn't you say?'

He nodded sagely. 'That's what I like about you. No nonsense. You see reality for what it is. God, I can live with that. Now, what about finance?'

'Finance?' she echoed.

'Yes. I'll call my solicitor and have a tentative partnership contract drawn up for you. I think a third share in Haywood Promotions would be fair for the mother of my child, don't you? That should give you a six-figure income every year. Of course, I'll also make you beneficiary of my life insurance policy in case anything untoward happens to me. And, naturally, I'll buy you a house. I'd like it to be not far from mine. I'll want to see as much of the baby as possible. But that can wait till you're well and truly pregnant. Oh, and I'll pay for a nanny or housekeeper or anything else you want as well. That is if you'd like to keep on working after the baby's born. Do you think you'll want to?'

Samantha's mind was reeling. As were her emotions. It was all really going to happen. A baby. She was actually going to have Guy's baby...

'Yes,' she said, trying not to sound as shaky as she felt. 'I would like to come back to work.'

'I thought you might,' he said, looking very satisfied with everything. 'You'll be able to bring the baby into the office with you sometimes. I'll enjoy minding him for you.'

Samantha tried not to gape. The mental image of Guy dandling a baby on his knee or changing nappies on the desk just didn't fit.

His laughter startled her. 'You don't have to look so shocked, Sam. I'm going to be a good father. In fact, a *great* father. Just as you're going to be a great mother. Hell, I couldn't have chosen better if I'd held auditions for the role. But now on to a more delicate matter, but an unavoidable one. I presume you're on the Pill?'

For a moment she was thrown till she realised he thought she'd been having a long-standing affair. 'No, I'm not,' she admitted.

He looked surprised, but pleased. 'Well, that's a bonus. No delay there, then. What about your periods? Are you regular? When was your last one?'

'Oh...I—er—um...a couple of weeks ago, I think.'

He gave her a mildly exasperated look. 'Can't you be more specific than that? Conceiving is not a hit and miss affair, you know. It's an exact science. Now think again. When exactly is your next period due?'

Samantha battled to keep a threatening blush from appearing. She flicked over her desk calendar in a pretence of looking at dates till she had herself under control again. 'Two weeks Sunday,' she stated with a return to cool efficiency. Thank the lord she *was* regular and it hadn't taken much thinking about. She needed all her brain power to keep her wits about her and stop Guy from finding out her secret.

He seemed eminently satisfied. 'What incredible timing! This means we don't have to waste this month. We can get started tonight.'

Her whole stomach somersaulted. '*Tonight*! But I can't! I mean...'

His face stiffened, his eyes hardening. Oh, God, she should have realised that, once having made a decision, he would want to be off and running. Guy was not a proscrastinator. He was a man of action. A doer.

'What do you mean, you can't?' he said sharply. 'You haven't got a date with that creep who won't marry you, have you? If you have, cancel it! There's no future there. Besides, *you* made the rules. No other lovers was the deal, wasn't it?'

She gulped. 'Yes.'

'Then that's settled? And in case you're worried about catching anything from me, put your mind at rest. I'm a very careful man.' He slid a speculative glance her way. 'I can't imagine you taking any unnecessary chances, but I suppose I should ask.'

'I have never been at risk,' she said. Norman had been as virginal as she had. As she still *was*, in an emotional sense.

'Can you be sure?' he persisted. 'This man you've been involved with—is he a swinger?'

She had difficulty keeping a straight face. 'You might describe him that way. But I...I've never actually slept with him.'

He was taken aback. 'But you said you had.'

'No, Guy,' she denied. 'I said I'd had a close relationship with him. But there's been no sexual intercourse.'

His frown was swift and dark and prolonged. 'You're not a virgin, are you, Sam?' he said at last.

She stiffened. 'No.'

'That's a relief,' he said, and Samantha wanted to hit him. She might have if there hadn't been a knock on the door at that moment.

Guy glanced at his watch. 'That'll be Rolf. Unfortunately I've just remembered I have a business dinner I can't get out of this evening, but I could meet you afterwards somewhere. I should be able to get away by nine-thirty. Look, we can decide on a suitable place to meet here in town after Rolf's gone. I can't think now.'

With that he walked briskly to the door, covering the reception area with athletic, confident strides. The door was yanked open. 'Come in, Rolf,' he said heartily, as though everything were nice and normal at Haywood Promotions. 'Great to see the sun shining, isn't it? Would you mind getting us some coffee, please, Sam? Some biscuits too. We have a lot of work to get through today and need some fortification.'

She grimaced as both men disappeared into the inner sanctum. *He* needed fortification? That was a laugh. The man was a machine, without sensitivity, without feelings, without *heart*! Why she loved him she couldn't fathom, but love him she did, madly, desperately. And tonight she was going to be able to express that love in the most intimate way.

Tonight...

Samantha glanced at the wall clock and groaned. It was going to be a long, long day.

CHAPTER FIVE

NINE twenty-five that evening found Samantha sitting at a table in the Sailor's Shanty restaurant, waiting agitatedly for Guy to arrive. She'd been there a full ten minutes, but he still wasn't late. He'd said nine-thirty. She hadn't planned to be early, but the taxi she'd caught had fairly whizzed into town, catching every green light on the way.

Her eyes flicked around the restaurant and adjoining cocktail bar, and she fancied it was probably a regular haunt of Guy's. A dimly lit affair, tucked into a side-street not far from Circular Quay, it had a cosy, intimate atmosphere suited to rendezvous with members of the opposite sex.

The décor was appropriate to its name: small wooden tables covered with checked tablecloths; plenty of ropes, nets and anchors hanging from the high-beamed ceilings; old lamps sitting on tea-chests in the corners. All the waiters were rigged out in sailor suits and the *maître d'* was dressed as a ship's captain with a dashing white uniform and cap.

Of course, the *pièce de résistance* was the dance-floor and the sultry singer playing at the piano in the corner. Already several couples were swaying in sensuous unison under hazy red lights, their hands and bodies making movements more like foreplay than dancing.

Samantha felt her throat going dry as she watched a particularly amorous pair drift close by her table. It reminded her forcibly of why she was here, why

67

she had gone to so much trouble with her appearance, why she was trembling inside with anticipation of the night ahead.

But she was also reminded of the inevitable consequences to what she was about to do. And, while Guy had convinced her of his sincerity at being a good father, Samantha knew that to embark on this course was to take a terrible risk with her future happiness. Could she cope with having Guy make love to her, then watch him move on to someone else? Could she cope with having him in her life, yet not really in it?

A waiter stopped by her table and asked again if she wanted a drink. Again she declined. She was too agitated to hold a glass, too nervous, too...

A sob caught in her throat and she closed her eyes tight. Oh, Guy... Guy... Do you have any idea how much I love you?

Emotion welled up inside her and she had to lean her elbows on the table and hide her face for a moment. Just in time she gathered herself, for as she straightened and opened her eyes she saw Guy making his way towards her across the smoke-filled room.

The lump was back in her throat as she watched him approach. For the sight of him had put the death-knell on any last-second urge to run away. She couldn't. She wanted him too much. She had to hold him in her arms, even if it was only for a few precious days and nights. At least afterwards she would have his child to love. Though right at this moment she couldn't seem to see that far ahead, or grasp such a reality.

She tried not to stare at him, looking far too handsome in a dashing charcoal suit and subtle ivory shirt, a flash of confident colour in the tur-

quoise tie and pocket handkerchief. Only his hair
defied his overall look of urbane elegance, a rebellious lock flopping down across his forehead.

At least she felt happy with her own appearance.
More than happy. She'd been quite excited by the
reflection that had flashed back at her in the mirror
just before she'd left home. Nevertheless, when Guy
drew up at their table and began surveying her
closely Samantha's chest tightened with that old
lack of confidence she used to feel as a teenager.

'Well, well,' he drawled, lifting a sardonic
eyebrow and pulling out a chair to sit down.
'Something tells me you've been hiding your light
under a bushel, Miss Peters.' His blue eyes sparkled
with dry amusement as they skated over the way
her normally restrained hair was now framing her
fully made-up face in an elegant mass of curls and
waves.

It had never occurred to Samantha that Guy
would find her improved appearance in any way
amusing, and it had a deflating effect. She had
hoped he would be pleasantly surprised by—even
turned on by—her 'new' self.

So much for all your hours of preparation,
dummy, she castigated herself privately.

Guy was definitely not *turned on* as he settled
back in his chair, his expression remaining at best
only mildly amused. His understated reaction
brought a degree of despair and a wealth of self-
anger, but Samantha knew that to reveal either was
out of the question.

Smothering her agitation with great difficulty, she
adopted an equally casual attitude, lifting her
shoulders in a nonchalant shrug. 'You've seen the
type of ad on TV, haven't you, Guy? Prim and
proper secretary goes home, takes down her hair,

whips off her glasses and tailored jacket, undoes the top three buttons on her blouse, sprays herself with perfume, and *voilà*—instant vamp!'

He chuckled. 'Not quite the same, I'm afraid. Firstly, you don't wear glasses, and while your hair has come down the buttons on your blouse are still firmly done up, I see.' He leant forward slightly and sniffed. 'The perfume is vampish, though. Yes . . . quite nice.'

If Samantha had had it with her she would have poured the whole bottle over his insensitive male head. *Quite nice*, she thought tartly. What sort of compliment was that? Didn't he know she wanted him to rave about how she looked? Tell her she was breathtakingly beautiful and could think of nothing but to take her home to bed this instant?

'It's called Seduction,' she stated with flat irony, recalling bitterly the high hopes that had inspired its purchase that afternoon on the way home.

High hopes! she scorned herself again. I couldn't turn this man on sexually if I stripped off my clothes and did the cancan on the table in front of him.

The mental image of her doing such a thing rather tickled her fancy, however, for her underwear *was* very French and blatantly sexy. Another of her afternoon purchases!

A wry smile tugged at her mouth. Perhaps he won't be so complacent when I do undress. The white lace bikini pants and suspender belt were supposed to be the latest in erotica. Or so the lady in the lingerie boutique had said. And the under-wired white lace bra she had on gave her a cleavage one could get lost in.

But then she remembered that Guy fancied the less endowed variety of bosom, and the little that was left of her female confidence went up in smoke.

Her attention swung resignedly back to Guy, who was leaning back in his chair and dragging away on his cigarette as though his life depended on it. The thought insinuated that, for all his apparent composure, he might be finding the prospect of their sleeping together as daunting as she was.

Good, she decided savagely, her feminine pride finding solace in vengeance.

It was at that point she decided not to do a darned thing to help smooth his way. He wanted a child, didn't he? He was the man, the hunter, the lover! Well, then, it was his job to do the hunting *and* the loving. Be damned if she was going to make things easier for the selfish, insensitive sod! If he'd had any common sense at all he would have fallen in love with her years ago and prevented all this nonsense!

Samantha sat there in mutinous silence, thinking that if she could have done so without embarrassment she would have gone to the ladies' room and put her hair back up, then wiped off all the make-up, the smoky eyeshadow, the mascara, the foundation, the blusher *and* the scarlet gloss lipstick! As for the perfume... She was suddenly finding its musky scent cloying and overpowering.

The silence between them lengthened, becoming decidedly awkward, and in the end it was Samantha who ended it. 'How did your business dinner go?' she asked bluntly. 'Did you get the contracts you wanted?' His dinner had been with the directors of a new and up and coming music recording company.

'No trouble,' he answered curtly.

Typical, she thought with a dry bitterness. When didn't he get what he wanted?

'Let's not talk shop tonight, Sam,' he said abruptly, and darted a sharp glance her way.

Well, goodness gracious me, she thought with some surprise. He *was* finding this as awkward as she was. The idea rather pleased her.

'What *do* you want to talk about?' she asked, almost mischievously. 'The weather? The state of the economy?'

His eyebrows bunched into an impatient frown. Clearly he disapproved of her light, bantering tone. 'The matter at hand,' he ground out.

Now it was Samantha's turn to bristle at *his* tone. He might be her boss at the office, but here... tonight... they were equals. Partners. She would *not* be snapped at.

'Oh? I wouldn't have said it was at hand,' she retorted in blithe defiance. 'Unless, of course, you intend making love to me on the dance-floor. That couple over there are doing their damnedest, that's for sure.'

Again his eyes snapped her way, glaring at her. 'I find your facetious attitude most unlike you, Sam. Having a baby together is a very serious business.'

'I'm well aware of that,' she returned coolly. 'Which reminds me, did you know that smoking lowers a man's sperm count?'

His hand froze on the cigarette at his lips.

'We don't want to do anything that will make my conceiving more difficult and time consuming, do we?' she added snakily.

His gaze was withering, to say the least, but then a reluctant admiration crept in, softening it. He shrugged and leant forward to stub out his cigarette in the glass ashtray, a slow wry grin coming to his mouth. 'That would, indeed, be a catastrophe,' he drawled.

Before Samantha could decide if he was being sarcastic or not he waved to a passing waiter, who came over immediately. Guy had that sort of effect on waiters.

Without deferring to her, he ordered a bottle of undoubtedly good claret and a plate of cheeses. But then, he already knew she liked claret. She had revealed as much once after he had come back from a trip to the Barossa Valley last year with cases of red wine and thrown a wine-tasting party.

The waiter departed hurriedly, as though his life depended on giving prompt service, and Guy relaxed back in his chair, his blue eyes watching her closely through the haze he himself had contributed to. 'Can you stay the night at my place?' he asked softly.

Her stomach curled over at the unexpected seductive quality in his voice, but she kept her eyes remarkably steady. A light little laugh tripped from her lips, obscuring any shakiness in her voice. 'I haven't brought an overnight bag with me, if that's what you mean.'

'I think you could manage without, don't you?' he murmured, the smile hovering on his lips turning decidedly wicked and sexy.

God, she had to admire his style! In a few seconds he had changed from brusque boss to the supreme Casanova, unruffled, superbly confident, dashingly suave. Her insides began to churn as she wondered what he had in store for her, what he had planned.

Because he would have a plan. Of that she was certain. Guy always had a plan. He didn't let things happen by chance. This subtle shift into his Don

Juan mode was only the first stage in what she would imagine was a complex strategy to have the night run oh, so smoothly.

The arrival of the bottle of claret took on a different perspective with the change in Guy's manner. Aha, Samantha thought cynically. *That* had been move number one. Some wine to soothe the female's nerves and dull her inhibitions. Or had move number one been the choice of this place all round? The soft lights, the sexy music, the general atmosphere of intimacy.

Yes, she thought with a surge of irritation. Yes... He had already been planning his moves at the office that afternoon, the callous, conniving, calculating devil! Yet he'd sounded so matter-of-fact when he'd suggested this place, so... businesslike!

She glared down at the table as he filled up her glass with wine, trying to get her resentment under control. You have no *right* to be annoyed with him, she tried telling herself. You took up his offer with open eyes. You even *made* the initial proposition. Stop being so juvenile, so... female! You knew this wouldn't be the complete fulfilment of your dreams. Be grateful that he *is* trying to make it seem romantic. Don't fight it. Go with the flow!

'Just what I need,' she said, sweeping up her goblet as soon as his hand retreated. 'Shall we toast your success tonight, then?'

Her perfectly innocent reference to his *business* success earlier in the evening brought a highly amused twinkle to his eyes. 'Let's not count our chickens before they hatch, Sam. We haven't been to bed yet.'

She couldn't help it. She blushed. Which was not at all sensible, under the circumstances. The unemotionally involved and down-to-earth Samantha

Peters would not blush. Luckily Guy didn't seem to notice in this dim light, and her with all her make-up on. Still, it annoyed her, making her determined not only to get her irrational pique under control but to act as blasé as he was.

'Oh, I'm not worried about *that*,' she quipped with an airy wave of her free hand. 'I'm sure you'll manage perfectly. You've had enough practice.'

He must have missed the bite in her last remark, for he laughed. 'Too true. Though this *is* a first for me tonight, given the situation.'

'You mean the first time you've taken a woman to bed you don't fancy?'

This time he didn't miss her underlying tartness, for his eyes snapped to hers. He looked puzzled, then thoughtful. 'No,' he said slowly. 'I meant the first time I'll be trying to make a woman pregnant.'

She looked away from his probing gaze and drank some wine, but she could still feel his eyes upon her.

'I think, Sam,' he said firmly, 'you'd better say now if this is beyond you, if you've changed your mind. It'll be too late in the morning. There'll be no question of an abortion where a child of mine is concerned, believe me.'

Her eyes jerked back to clash with his, her expression one of proud dignity. 'Nor mine.'

They glared at each other for a moment. Then he smiled, disarmingly, winningly. 'That's what I like about you, Sam. You have courage, and spirit. We'll make a fine baby together, won't we?' He lifted his glass in recognition of that fact and drank.

A tiny whimper fluttered up into her throat, but she caught it just in time. She was grateful to be able to drop her eyes and concentrate on the wine. That way he wouldn't see the wild array of emotions that must have flashed through her eyes at his words. The joy. The love. The utter despair...

Lowering her glass to the table, she picked up a square of cheese and ate it with robotic precision.

'And you're wrong about my not fancying you,' he went on suavely. 'Looking as lovely as you do tonight, you'd be fancied by any man.'

Samantha's chin rose as she drew in a deep breath and let it out slowly. She found no real pleasure or credibility in his words. They sounded too slick, too pat to be true. Not to mention far too late. If anything, she felt disappointed that he thought he could fool her so easily.

'That's good,' she said, smiling a bitter little smile. 'Now all you have to do is make *me* fancy *you.*'

The words tumbled out of her mouth without deliberate intent, but, having said them, Samantha could hardly take them back. Besides, she found some solace for her damaged pride in seeing his astonishment. Clearly such an idea had never entered his head. Guy Haywood, lover *el supremo*! God's gift to the women of Sydney! Who would ever have imagined that there'd be a female between sixteen and sixty not prepared to drop to her knees before him! Samantha found surprising satisfaction in watching his momentary disconcertment. It spurred her on.

'Oh, I forgot,' she added with a sigh. 'Silly me. I don't really have to be turned on, do I? I suppose I can just lie there and endure.' She managed to sound both relieved and slightly bored at the same time.

Now he was really offended. His chin shot up and his eyes blazed. There was no doubting that the image of any lover of his being bored or 'enduring' beneath him went against Guy's grain. 'You find the prospect of going to bed with me that un-appealing?' he asked brusquely, and with an over-riding air of disbelief.

'Well ... let's just say I haven't looked upon you sexually before,' she lied, quite enjoying his dis-comfort now. The boot was well and truly on the other foot. 'I've never believed in mixing business with pleasure. In fact, it's a hard and fast rule with me. I mean, you're my *boss*, not my boyfriend, and, despite your undoubted—er—physical ... attractions, I am finding it hard to make the mental adjustment from employer to lover.' She gave an elaborate sigh. 'Not only that, Guy, but even if a girl *isn't* in love with a man when she goes to bed with him she does like her sex mixed with a certain amount of chemistry and romance, otherwise it can be quite ... unpalatable ...'

'*Unpalatable*!' he squawked.

'Hush, Guy, people are looking!' She sighed again. 'Of course, I can always just pretend if I have to. I do realise it's harder for you than for me. You *can't* pretend. Still ... I'm sure you'll manage ... But don't worry ...' her smile was mag-nificently bland as she lifted the wine glass once more ' ... I'm not expecting any miracles.'

He gave her a look back that showed she had gone a smidgeon too far. *More* than a smidgeon. No one threw down a challenge like that to Guy Haywood and got away with it. He swept his glass to his lips and drank with barely contained an-noyance, but when he lowered the glass to the table his eyes had cooled to an expression of superb con-fidence, and an enigmatic smile was hovering around his lips. 'That's good,' he agreed in a low voice that sent a prickle running up and down her spine. 'I've never believed in miracles myself. I'm more a God-help-those-who-help-themselves person. Shall we dance?'

Samantha's stomach flipped over. Her childish sparring match was over. Guy had picked up her gauntlet and she knew from experience that her boss was never a loser. He was going to use every ounce of his considerable skill and expertise as a lover to make sure there was not a hint of 'enduring' in their sexual encounters. He was setting out to capture not her heart—for he had no interest in hearts—but her body. Totally. Thoroughly. Completely.

The thought brought instant excitement. For *his* winning was *her* winning, she realised with heart pounding and blood racing. It was what she wanted, what she had set out to achieve, however unconsciously. Of course, he didn't know that he already had her heart anyway, or that her body could not be separated from it. But she imagined, naïvely perhaps, that what he didn't know wouldn't hurt him. Maybe it would have been wiser for her to worry about how such a fact might hurt *her*.

But Samantha was beyond such thoughts at that moment. Her throat went dry as she watched him rise to his feet, watched his eyes narrow sexily, watched his mouth curve back in an inviting smile. 'Come,' he said, and held out his hand.

For a second she hesitated, struck by a sudden suspicion that his invitation to dance masked a deeper more insidious invitation; one that would place herself not just in his arms, but in his control, her will surrendered to his, her life irrevocably in his hands.

Samantha wanted Guy, wanted his body and his child. She did not want his becoming her master, either sexually or any other way. Yet the power of desire was very strong, tempting her, seducing her. Coupled with her love for him, it was overwhelming. Stop worrying, it whispered persuasively. Stop thinking. Place your hand in his and just enjoy!

No, no, the voice of common sense groaned as her palm found his. Think of tomorrow, the future. Once he impregnates you with his child, there'll be no escape, no resignation, no running away. You'll be his, yet not his, forever. For pity's sake, don't do this. *Don't*!

Her hand gave one last tremor as his strong fingers closed around her. Her heart began to thud.

Too late... Too late...

She rose slowly to her feet, her eyes lifting to his. They held her so easily with their penetrating blue, their wicked intent, their steely confidence.

His gaze flicked over her full-length, with Samantha so besotted by him at that moment that she no longer questioned the admiration his eyes projected. A minute ago she might have scorned it for the deliberate ploy it obviously was.

Now, however, her foolish female heart embraced his admiration with an innocent delight. Now that she was standing up, she reasoned, he could really appreciate her transformed appearance, the subtle sexiness of her white chiffon blouse, with its full, flowing sleeves which gathered into narrow cuffs and its dainty crystal buttons at her wrists and down the front. There was no doubt in her mind that he was thinking her black pleated silk culottes suited her leggy figure and slim ankles to perfection and that he was simply mad about the scarlet silk scarf she'd tied around her waist as a final touch.

'Shades of buccaneer days, Sam?' he asked, amusement in his voice.

With difficulty she managed a small smile in return, but no words.

'It suits you,' he pronounced, and drew her into his arms.

Ridiculous of her to freeze at this point, to be besieged by a thousand fluttering fears. But she was. With a frown on his face Guy propelled her stiff, ungiving body on to the dance-floor, where he persevered for a few seconds before stopping with an impatient sigh. 'This does require some co-operation, Sam,' he rebuked under his breath.

Without waiting for an answer his hands refound the small of her back, feeling like burning brands on her chilled skin as they pressed her close to him. 'Put your arms up around my neck,' he suggested tersely. 'Pretend if you must, pretend I'm...that idiot man you're in love with, the one who doesn't want you.'

She flashed him a startled look. How right he was. At this very second, her body moulded to his like a second skin, she knew that idiot man certainly *didn't* want her. Not even one itty bitty little bit!

'I'm not very good at faking it,' she said tautly. '*Try*!'

She shrugged resignedly and did as he asked, sliding her arms up around his neck, shocking herself when a shudder of sensation reverberated all through her as her fingertips brushed the warm flesh above his collar. Shaken, she stilled her fingers.

'Relax,' he growled. 'Let yourself go.'

She closed her eyes and made a conscious effort not to worry about her reaction to him, to let the tension flow from her body. Do what he said, she ordered herself. Pretend... Pretend he loves you, wants you. Your dancing together is a prelude to a night of mad passion, the fulfilment of all your dreams.

It was so easy, once she had let go of reality, once her mind had glazed over and given her entry into that fantasy world where Guy did love her and want her, where she could do all the things she ached to do with him.

Her actions came automatically, naturally. First one of her hands rested lightly on his collar, the fingers of her other hand splaying up into his hair, her fingertips gently massaging his scalp in sensual abandon. Her face nestled under his chin, warm lips sipping at his skin with soft, moist kisses. Her whole body sank into his, her hips swaying more invitingly against his. Her mouth finally encountered and nibbled at an earlobe.

'Hell,' he muttered. And jerked back.

But not before she had felt the involuntary leap in his flesh.

They stared at each other, Samantha's hazel eyes still dilated with desire, Guy's wide with surprise... and anger. 'The man must be a bloody fool,' he snarled. 'So are you, Sam, to waste such passion on him.'

'I... I...'

'Never mind,' he growled impatiently. 'At least I know now how to turn you on. And me with it. Let's get out of here.'

CHAPTER SIX

FIVE minutes later Samantha was being bundled into a taxi outside the restaurant. Guy did own a car—the latest Nissan sports coupé—but around the city he preferred taxis. No parking problems. Less hassle all round.

She shivered as she settled into a corner of the vinyl seat.

'Cold?' Guy asked as the taxi accelerated away.

'A little,' she admitted.

'Here...' He slid an arm around her shoulders and scooped her over against his body warmth.

Samantha shivered again. Not from the cold this time.

'I would have thought a sensible girl like you would have brought a coat,' Guy reprimanded softly.

'We all make mistakes,' she said coolly, returning instinctively to the aloof, controlled façade that had been her protection all her life. Amazon Sam had never shown emotion or upset over her schoolfriends' gibes, despite feeling crippled inside. The adult Samantha Peters had fallen madly in love with her boss, yet gone about her job efficiently, and no one had guessed her inner torment. Now, on her way to that same boss's bedroom, she was so nervous that she had to lock her agitation within a steely armour or fall apart.

On that dance-floor, when Guy had urged her to let down her guard, she had momentarily become the woman she really was beneath the composed exterior, passionate and emotional and devastatingly in love, a woman who yearned and felt with a frightening intensity. How on earth was she going to get through a night of real lovemaking without betraying her secret? One intimate touch from Guy and her façade was sure to crumble, with her heart exposed.

Her only hope, she decided in desperation, was to rigidly cling to her cool, calm demeanour when Guy wasn't making love to her, then use the excuse he had already given her when he *was*—that of pretending another man was in bed with her, that her passion was not for Guy, but her secret lover.

It seemed a perverse twist of fate that Guy had been turned on by her actions during her brief loss of control, that he would never know *he* was the man she loved. The bitter irony of the situation was not lost on Samantha, but she had no alternative but to keep up the charade.

'Won't be long,' Guy assured her when she gave another little shudder, 'and we'll be in the warmth of an air-conditioned bedroom.'

The word 'bedroom' was all she heard. She closed her eyes and tried hard not to think of anything, to blank out all her thoughts. Her mind, though, had ideas of its own, most of which were filled with white lace lingerie and hard male flesh and fantasies fulfilled. A quiet heat began to creep through her body.

The taxi jerked to a stop at the kerb outside the high security wall that surrounded Guy's place, forcing Samantha to snap out of her dreaming. She slid an agitated glance over at Guy, who was paying the driver with his usual unhurried ease. No nerves for him now, she thought ruefully. The problem of their sexual compatability had been solved. *She* had solved it for him on the dance-floor.

'Here. Take my hand,' he offered, and drew her out of the taxi on to the chilly pavement.

She extracted her hand as soon as possible but without making a fuss. Nevertheless her action drew a lifted eyebrow from Guy. He shrugged and determinedly put an arm around her shoulder instead, keeping her close to his side as he led her over to the security gate, keys already in his free hand.

Guy's home was no secret to Samantha in the main. She had been to it several times before and was no longer in awe of its opulence and ultra-modern décor. Without a word passing between them, Guy shepherded her through the security gate, up the pebble-covered driveway, through the huge double front doors, across the black slate foyer, up the gleaming chrome staircase and along the grey carpeted corridor to his bedroom door.

At this point her familiarity with the layout ended. She had never been in his bedroom before.

He flung the door open and waved her inside with a flourish and an enigmatic smile.

She swallowed and forced her legs to propel her by now overwrought self forwards. The door shut softly behind her.

With one sweeping glance Samantha realised that 'bedroom' was a highly inadequate word for the area of the house that constituted Guy's private sleeping quarters. No presidential suite could have been larger, or more luxurious, no boudoir more completely set up for entertaining 'guests'.

In the immediate area there was an enormous sitting-room, complete with suitably dim side-lamps, a bar, a hi-fi system, a new flat-screened television and a video machine. Behind the strategically placed and very deeply cushioned sofas, open double doors led to an equally large room, this one housing an enormous bed on a slightly raised carpeted platform. Further on, one whole wall was plate glass, leading out on to a discreet and very private balcony with a view of black sky and stars above the harbour.

Samantha glimpsed a huge *en suite* bathroom through another open door, and didn't need to inspect it to know it would have every possible mod-con, including a spa bath. She had difficulty hiding what she thought of such an obvious place, masking her distaste behind a bland face that she suspected was still a fraction disapproving.

Yet really she had no right to feel surprised by or critical of such a layout, she told herself frankly. It was no less than was to be expected from the prince of affairs. Naturally, he would want somewhere beautiful and functional in which to conduct his...liaisons.

Again she gave a small grimacing shudder, though quickly bringing herself to task when she saw Guy frowning over at her from where he was standing behind the bar.

Truly, Samantha, came the stern voice of common sense and fairness. You're becoming a fraction holier than thou, aren't you? You've always known what he was, and he didn't *force* you to come here. He's even given you plenty of opportunity to back out.

Yet you *are* here. And one of the reasons you are is because of this very room, in a way. Guy's sexual appetite—his obvious capacity to enjoy women—was part of his appeal, wasn't it? Why object to what was, after all, an integral part of his personality? Stop being a hypocrite and say something before he thinks there's something wrong with you and changes *his* mind.

'I didn't realise you liked blue so much,' she remarked in what sounded like a perfectly normal voice. Nearly everything in the suite of rooms was blue, from the palest shade in the carpet to a rich royal on his bed. 'The rest of the house is fairly neutral.'

He glanced up from where he was busy opening a bottle of champagne. 'If you recall, the house came already decorated,' he replied casually. 'I did make some changes, but I liked these rooms the way they were. I find blue a very restful colour.'

'I doubt much resting is done in here,' she muttered, giving way to one last surge of irritation.

'What was that?' He frowned.

'I said I think blue's restful too.' She put her handbag down and wandered over to stand behind a sofa but could not stay still, moving on to the open doorway leading to the bedroom. She stood there awkwardly and began to fidget with her fingers.

He darted her a brief, surveying glance, then shook his head, his mouth curving into a sardonic smile as his eyes dropped again to the bottle. What on earth was he thinking? she worried with a surge of insecurity. That she was plain beneath all the war-paint? Too tall? Too big? Gauche, even? Not a patch on Debra?

Perhaps. Probably. God, but this was worse than she'd imagined. If only there hadn't been any delay after what had happened between them at the restaurant. If only he'd got straight on with it. She didn't want a drink. She wanted him to take her in his arms, kiss her, lie to her, make her forget that she would never be his choice of lover, that his taking her to bed was only a means to an end.

At last the champagne was poured, and he carried two fluted glasses towards her, his eyes amused. 'You look as if you could do with this. You're prowling around like a cat on a hot tin roof.'

'What do you expect?' she burst out suddenly, irritated by his insensitivity. 'This is hardly what I do every Friday night, you know.'

He stopped in his tracks, his eyes hardening.

'I'm sorry,' she groaned. 'I'm being silly, I suppose, but I do wish you'd get on with it, Guy. I can't stand the waiting. It's driving me mad.'

His laughter was very, very dry as he came forward and pressed a glass into her hand. 'I'd like to think you were madly impatient for my body, but something tells me your feelings are rather more... theatrical.'

'*Theatrical*?' She blinked her confusion up at him. What on earth did he mean? That she was acting?

'As in an operating theatre,' he elaborated as they both sipped the champagne. 'You reek of the I-can't-wait-to-get-it-over-with attitude. Hardly flattering, dear Sam.' His tone had a frustrated edge to it. 'What happened to that girl I was dancing with, eh? That warm, sensual creature who kissed my neck and played with my hair and sent me into a spin. Do you think she could be revived?'

He didn't wait for her to answer. He took the glass back from her tremulous hand and placed it with his on a side-table, then, without saying another word, tipped her chin up with the finger-tips of one hand. For a second he hesitated, and she closed her eyes, her heart in her mouth.

The kiss didn't eventuate, however, and when she finally opened her eyes it was to find him glaring down at her. 'I may be an arrogant fool,' he muttered, 'but do you think we could try this *without* your pretending I'm someone else this time? Leave your eyes open, Sam,' he rasped. '*Watch* who's kissing you. Who knows? You might find you like it.'

There was a wealth of controlled anger in the way his fingers closed on her chin. Not hard enough to bruise, but still very firm, brooking no opposition in this. His head descended very slowly, his gaze never leaving hers. His mouth touched, tormented, then lifted. His eyes had grown oddly dark and there was a flash of red across his cheeks. Samantha wasn't too calm either, her breathing decidedly disjointed and a buzzing in her ears.

'See?' he husked. 'Was that so bad?'

He bent and kissed her again, moving his mouth with more pressure over hers, then parting his lips, taking hers with him, his tongue probing forward. An electric current charged through her body and she shuddered violently.

'Goddammit!' Guy snarled, and whirled away from her. He stood for a second, his back to her, hands on hips, his sigh heavy and exasperated. He swept up his glass of champagne and downed half of it, then, putting it back down, turned slowly to face her.

'Right,' he pronounced, his momentary annoyance no longer in evidence. But his eyes carried that stubborn look they got whenever he was presented with a problem and was determined to solve it in his own inimitable way.

'I can see you need your pretence,' he went on reasonably. 'I'll have to accept that. But I find your squeezing your eyes shut, very...offputting. If you must have a fantasy world to help you then let me suggest something a little more...mutually satisfying. OK, Sam?'

She had no idea what he was talking about but she nodded dumbly. If it was to give her an out then she was all for it. My God, when his tongue had slid into her mouth just now she had been virtually galvanised with blistering sensation. How would she be later, when he really started making love to her? Ironic, though, of him to ask her permission to do anything at this point. Little did he know it but she was his to do with as he willed.

She was still startled, however, when he reached forward and undid the silk sash at her waist, then shocked her to the core by blindfolding her with it. 'What...what are you doing?' she gasped, her hands fluttering upwards in defence, only to have them grabbed and forcibly held behind her back.

'Trust me, Sam,' he said firmly. 'Don't be frightened.'

'But I am frightened,' she whispered, the sudden blackness and imprisoning grip of his hands sending a wave of heat flooding through her. She had heard of games like this, sensual games of captive playing, of the woman acting out the role of a slave in bondage. But she had never envisaged doing it herself. Or liking it. Yet she was definitely excited, her heartbeat pumping away like a steam train in full throttle.

He released her wrists to cradle her face in his hands. '*Trust* me,' he insisted, and lightly kissed her quavering mouth.

'All...all right.'

His hands dropped from her and she was left standing there, feeling bereft, and awkward. 'What... what are you doing?'

'Taking off my jacket and shirt. It's warm in here.'

'Oh...' Her mind shot back to that day in the office when he had stripped to the waist in front of her. The thought that he was doing that now sent a searing heat into her skin. Her cheeks were burning. *She* was burning.

The seconds ticked by and she could hear the faint sounds of clothes being discarded. He wasn't taking them *all* off, was he? If he did surely he'd put a robe on, not just walk around like... like...?

Suddenly she couldn't bear the uncertainty, the darkness. She had to know what he was doing, what was happening. Hands trembling uncontrollably, they lifted to the knot.

'Don't!' he commanded instantly, his hands closing over hers, taking them down. 'Don't,' he repeated in a raw whisper, and placed her hands on his bare chest.

They jerked away as though stung by an electric shock. 'You're naked!' she accused, voice shaking.

'No,' he soothed, sliding his arms around her waist and drawing her to him. 'I've still got my trousers on. See?'

'I... I can't see,' she reminded him in a daze of erotic excitement.

'Feel, then.'

'Yes,' she gulped. 'Yes...' Dear God, but it was what she had always wanted to do, ached to do. To touch him at will, to feel him, to let her hands speak her love. They fluttered back to his flesh, revelling in the warm supple skin that covered his shoulders, sliding backwards and forwards, kneading, feeling, wanting. She sighed and bent her mouth to his chest, savouring the slight roughness of hair under her lips.

She felt his shudder of pleasure and exulted in it, exulted in the strong male hands that shook slightly when they cupped her throat and lifted her chin upwards. 'Give me your mouth, Sam,' he ground out. 'And no flinching this time...'

Her mouth reached up, her lips parting in eager readiness.

There was certainly no shudder, only delight and hunger and passion. She accepted his kiss avidly, thrilling to the blasts of fire that burnt into her brain every time his tongue plunged deep into her mouth. Yes, she thought. Yes... This is what I've always known it would be like with him. Now I want it all.

He drew back from her at last and she could hear his breathing, as ragged and heavy as her own. The knowledge of his arousal sparked even more within herself. She clung back to him, lifting her face for more, but he took her shoulders and held her firmly away.

'No more of that.' Despite everything, his voice sounded stunningly controlled. It rocked her, this power he had to gather himself at any time. But then she remembered that *he* wasn't being swept along by love. This was just sex. Sex with a purpose. He only needed to be sufficiently aroused so that he could successfully make love to her and conceive a child.

'Time to move on,' he said curtly.

She knew what he meant the moment she felt his fingers on the buttons of her blouse. He was going to undress her, standing there in the centre of a lighted room. The thought kept taunting her that

she was not his choice, that her body was not the
sort that normally attracted him, that he had needed
an erotic game to turn him on. Swamped by a
sudden loss of confidence, she made a whimpering
protest. 'No, I ... Please turn off the lights.'

'No,' was his simple denial.

Despite the scarf, she squeezed her eyes shut as
his fingers worked their way steadily down the front
of her blouse. They weren't easy buttons to undo,
being square-cut glass. But Guy didn't appear to
have much trouble, except perhaps at her wrist, and
even they gave way quickly. She held herself stiffly
as he parted the blouse and slipped it off her
shoulders.

His sharp intake of breath came as something of
a surprise, till she started imagining he found her
full breasts repulsive. She had always been rather
proud of them, had thought the lacy half-cup bra
had made them look extra voluptuous and sexy,
but as she endured Guy's silence she began to believe she had the ugliest bosom in the world.

When her hands lifted instinctively to cover
herself they were pushed away. 'Don't be silly,' he
ground out. 'You have beautiful breasts, Sam.
Exquisite...'

She swayed when she felt his touch on them,
tracing lightly at first, fingertips only, but when she
experienced the full heat of his open palms
moulding over the bra cups a tremor shook her.
His thumbs started rubbing across the tips with
slow, tantalising rolling movements. She thought
she would die from pleasure, her nipples springing
erect and sensitive against the lace, her body gripped
by the most amazing sexual tension.

'Such deliciously...large...sensitive nipples,' he
said in a voice she scarcely recognised as his. It was

definitely not quite under control. The knowledge that the sight of her body could stir him to lose his much vaunted composure brought both satisfaction and a sense of incredible power. She, Sam, his long-ignored secretary, could make his voice tremble, could make his fingers quiver. Maybe at last he would see that she could give him as much as any of his blondes. More even, if he would only let her love him as she wanted to love him. She would show him passion he had never dreamed existed in his emotionally devoid, casually sexual lifestyle. She would pleasure him, give him what every man wanted in a woman. Total willingness, absolute submission, complete surrender.

But I can't go that far, she thought frantically. I mustn't. He's far too intuitive. He might guess the truth. I mustn't moan, even though his touch is driving me to distraction, even though I want to ask him—no beg him—to do more. I mustn't. I mustn't...

If only he hadn't chosen that moment to unhook the front-closing clasp of her bra and draw the garment from her, hadn't put his hands back on her throbbing breasts, bent his lips to take a single tortured nipple into the hot cavern of his mouth. She not only moaned. She gasped in a series of dragged-in, shuddering breaths, arching her back in utter abandonment and ecstasy. Unbidden, love-filled words slipped into her whirling, chaotic mind. 'Oh, my darling...my darling...' Samantha was so enraptured, so aroused, that she wasn't even aware the endearments had found voice.

She vaguely heard his muttered oath, but when his hands and mouth deserted her abruptly she wondered hopelessly why he had done such a thing.

'You ... you can't stop now,' she pleaded huskily, her hands fluttering in bewilderment in front of her.

He grasped them to his chest and crushed them mercilessly till she whimpered. 'Guy! You're hurting me.'

He laughed and made no concession to his brutal hold. 'Well, at least you know it's *me* who's doing the hurting, not your damned darling.'

'Darling?' she repeated, muddled for a second. Then she realised what she must have done and her cheeks scorched with heat. 'I ... I'm sorry ... It's just that ...'

'Yes, yes,' he bit out frustratedly, flinging her hands away from him. 'But, for pity's sake, Sam, it's a bit hard for a man to take, to have a woman groaning for her lover while *he's* making love to her.'

'He ... he's not my lover,' she rasped. Not yet anyway, she thought in wild desperation.

'But you want him to be, don't you? You want him with a want I've never seen before in a woman.' He grabbed her shoulders and shook her. 'Who is this man who commands such desire, such love? Do I know him? Tell me!'

She was startled by the vehemence in his voice, the violence in his hands. He actually sounded jealous, madly jealous. And, even though she knew it was only his insufferable male ego that was being piqued, she found satisfaction in his passion. She would use his anger, his temper, pretend it was all for her and her alone.

'Don't question me, Guy,' she rasped, winding her arms up around his neck and pulling him down to her. 'Just touch me, kiss me, take what *he* doesn't want, take it.'

He groaned, but did as she asked, bending his mouth to hers, kissing her till she was limp with desire, till her mouth ached with his ravaging onslaughts, till her breasts were pulsating orbs of bruised flesh, till she was begging him to stop, to stop and make love to her properly.

He ripped the scarf from her eyes and she saw a Guy such as she had never seen before, his face flushed with dark blood, his eyes wild and frightening. She stared up at him, her own eyes widening with shock. So this was the man who obsessed all those women, this impassioned, primitive animal who was as far removed from the controlled person she worked with as night was from day.

They were well matched, this man and herself, she thought with bitter acceptance. Both fools who wore façades, but for different reasons. Hers to mask the vulnerabilities of her emotions, his to hide the raw male passion that could so easily consume and rule his life if he let it. But, as of this moment, both their façades had been blasted to smithereens.

Their eyes locked and she was amazed to see a type of bewilderment creep into his, and, with the bewilderment, anger. He didn't like her seeing him like this, didn't like it one bit. Gradually and amazingly he regained control over himself, his breathing forcibly steadied with deep, heaving breaths, cooling his passion and his anger till he had successfully achieved the impossible: total control. He'd even adopted a faintly sardonic expression.

'You're a wild little thing, aren't you, Sam,' he drawled, 'once you get going?' His hands reached out to casually cup her lush breasts, lifting and kneading them slowly while he watched her lips part in a gasping moan. His eyes narrowed and she felt his fingers dig into her flesh before abruptly dropping his hands away. They slowly encircled her waist, where his expert fingers casually undid the buttons at the back of her culottes. Her eyes rounded, her breath catching in her throat as he slid the zip down with one sleek movement.

'Tell me,' he murmured while he eased the culottes down over her hips, 'how far exactly have you gone with this wimpish lover of yours? Has he kissed you, touched you, made you quiver with pleasure, as I have just done? Have you touched his flesh, given him satisfaction while he denies you yours? Is that why you're so frustrated? For that's what you are...' Intuitive blue eyes were fixed on her dilated gaze. 'Incredibly so...'

How could she answer him when her world was whirling about her? He was undressing her, the man she loved. Dear God, she was only human...

She sucked in a shuddering breath and shook her head, masking her eyes from him by looking down.

'Don't do that!' he commanded. 'Look up at me!'

Drawn by the power in his voice, she lifted her face.

'No more pretence, Sam,' he growled, eyes steely and narrow. 'Time for reality. Soon you'll be naked in my bed and we'll be making love. I won't have a ghost in bed with us. Not this time. Tonight you are *my* woman, the woman I have chosen to be the mother of my child. I won't share you.'

The culottes fell from her hips and pooled at her feet. He stared down at her, frozen for a second as his eyes raked over her erotic attire. But then he smiled, and there was more than a hint of smugness in his beautiful blue eyes.

'Dare I remind you, Sam,' he drawled, taking her hand and stepping her out of the circle of black silk, 'that you must have worn these for me, for no other man was going to see you like this tonight? An interesting thought, that, wouldn't you say?'

She stared up at him, eyes wide, lips apart as she sucked in some much needed air.

'I'm certainly going to enjoy taking them off,' he rasped, and bent to scoop her up into his arms, carrying her into his bedroom and laying her quite tenderly on the royal-blue quilt.

Nervous shivers racked her body as he unclipped first one suspender, then the other. But he didn't seem to notice, his attention riveted on her legs as he unpeeled each stocking from her and removed the last of her clothing. Only when she was totally naked did he look up into her eyes, shocking her with the undisguised admiration in his gaze.

'You are one beautiful woman, Sam,' he murmured, and bent to lightly kiss each one of her nipples before abruptly standing up and stepping down from the bed.

'Where...where are you going?' she gasped.

He threw a reassuring smile over his shoulder. 'To the bathroom. I won't be a minute. Pop into bed if you like.'

She did like. To lie there in outstretched nudity, waiting patiently for his return, was out of the question. She scrambled under the sheets, aware that she had begun to tremble from nerves. Once again, at the critical moment, he had left her alone, allowing her arousal to recede enough for doubts and worries to crowd back in. Would he realise her inexperience? Would he find her inept and boring? Would she rate poorly as a woman, compared with all his other exciting, sophisticated lovers?

As she lay there agitatedly her whirling thoughts took a different turn. Would making love with Guy end in the ultimate in physical satisfaction that women seemed to talk about these days and want so desperately? She wasn't sure what orgasm was like, or how a woman felt when she experienced it. All she knew was that she wanted Guy back with her again; wanted to have him touch her, kiss her, caress her; wanted him to complete what he had started. The thought of their two bodies blending as one was enough to blast a heat wave across her skin, her heart leaping, her breath coming in shallow pants as she merely imagined it. What would the reality do to her?

The door to the *en suite* opened and Guy wandered back in. Samantha gulped, for not in any shape or form had her experience with Norman prepared her for seeing a man like Guy, stunningly naked and breathtakingly aroused.

He seemed pleased by her undivided attention as he strolled over, lifted the bedclothes and climbed in beside her. 'I think,' he said, and reached to enfold her against him, 'that this is going to work out much better than I'd envisaged. Though the fact is, Sam...' he leant over her and held her flushing face solid in his hands '...I don't think I can wait much longer.'

Nevertheless, he did, kissing her and touching her and caressing her as she'd yearned for, bringing her arousal right back to fever-pitch, making her flesh quiver and tremble till she could no longer contain her moans of pure sensual pleasure. When he eased her thighs apart and started to touch her with even more intimacy she was soon beside herself, her body arching up from the bed in its desire to get closer and closer to him.

'Now, I think,' he muttered at last, and positioned himself between her thighs, wrapping her legs around his hips before he probed at the silken sheath he had so expertly prepared. She gasped in anticipation, her nails digging into his shoulders. As though in response to her action, he simultaneously thrust forward, totally destroying any concept she had of what it might feel like to be thus joined with the man she loved. This wasn't the stuff heaven was made of. This was hell, for she knew she would never want to be without it again.

Emotion sent a strangled sob to her throat and tears to her eyes. She nestled her face in his neck, terrified he would see her tears, and know them for what they were.

But then he began to move and she groaned, stunned by the exquisite physical pleasure of it all.

'Move with me, Sam,' he urged.

She did, grasping him tight and close, searching to devour him with an all-consuming ardour.

'Hell,' he muttered once.

She felt the changes in her body, felt the gradual increasing of tension, the relentless tightening of her internal muscles, but had no idea where they were leading. Eventually her fingers began to dig deeply into Guy's back and a tortured moan punched from her throat. Perhaps sensing her imminent release, Guy scooped his hands under her buttocks and lifted her into him, his penetration more devastatingly complete.

She climaxed immediately, her back arching from the bed as her body was gripped by contraction after contraction of sheer electric pleasure.

She clasped Guy to her, thrilling when she felt his responsive shudder, felt his body convulsing with hers in perfect unity.

More tears flooded her eyes. Tears of joy and bitter-sweet happiness.

'Oh, Guy,' she sobbed, and clung to him.

He stiffened, jerking his head up to stare down at her.

There was no way she could do anything about the tears that were running down her cheeks.

'The bastard,' he muttered. 'The stupid bloody bastard...' And then he was gathering her to him, holding her and stroking her, telling her she was a beautiful woman, a beautiful, desirable, wonderful woman and she was to forget that other fool, forget him, put him out of her mind forever. He didn't deserve her love, didn't deserve a minute of her time.

Which only made her cry the more.

In the end she sobbed herself to sleep, still locked in his arms, unaware that she wasn't the only person in that room to be experiencing an emotional upheaval.

Guy lay awake for a long, long time, cradling her sleeping form, thinking about what had happened. Every now and then Samantha stirred, sighing contentedly as he stroked her gently back to oblivion. Each time it happened he frowned darkly, aware of instant tension leaping back into his body whenever her soft lips pressed instinctively into his neck. It bothered him, as did all the other emotions that had besieged him that night.

'Impossible,' he muttered aloud at last, his eyes hardening.

And, as though that were the end of the matter, he promptly turned away from her and went to sleep.

CHAPTER SEVEN

SAMANTHA woke first, slowly, sleepily. Her eyes finally fluttered open, widening when she saw the foot of the bed bathed in light.

All that had happened the night before flooded back, as sharply as the sun's rays that were streaming through the plate-glass window above her head. Rolling over carefully, her wide hazel eyes took in Guy's sleeping form. He was well over on his side, his back to her, the pale blue sheet draped carelessly around his hips.

Her breathing quickened as her gaze followed the shape of his body upwards, the indentation at his waist, the rapidly broadening chest, the wide, very male shoulders, the strong muscles in his neck, the tangled mass of thick straight brown hair, looking longer than it did when neatly groomed around his head.

Would she remember what he looked like naked in years to come? came the suddenly bleak thought. Would she be able to recapture for her private dream-world his incredible passion, his unexpected tenderness towards her afterwards?

'Don't let me get pregnant too quickly, lord,' she prayed softly under her breath. 'Give me a few months of happiness, of feeling like this, like a woman loved, a woman in every sense of the word.'

She sighed, and stretched her arms languorously above her head, savouring the contentment in her body. Yet no sooner had she begun to think she

was at peace, at least physically, than her remi-
niscing had a stirring effect, teasing her brain with
memories of what had transpired between them.
She closed her eyes and began to relive those
amazing moments from when she'd been standing
before him, blindfolded and half naked, when his
hands had . . .

Her eyes snapped open as a surge of desire struck
deep and hard. My God, she thought frantically.
I'm *worse*, not better! I want him more now than
ever!

Stifling a groan, she eased her legs over the side
of the bed and sat up, pushing her own tangled mass
of hair out of her eyes. A shower, she decided, and,
giving Guy's still unconscious state a grateful
glance, gingerly transported her naked self from the
bed to the bathroom.

She stayed under the hot water longer than strictly
necessary, considering she wasn't shampooing her
hair. But the alternative was facing Guy. She imagined he would probably have been awakened by
the sound of the gushing jets of water by now.

Uncertainty and a residue of shyness squirmed
through Samantha as she envisaged emerging from
the room to encounter his knowing gaze. She had
no idea what he would want of her for the rest of
the weekend, whether he expected her to stay with
him for the whole two days, or how often he would
make love to her. She tried not to think too deeply
about this last matter, for it had the effect of
making her drop the soap and generally lose what
little composure she was desperately trying to find.

It was imperative that she keep her resolve of last
night, that of being her usual cool self when they
were out of bed. One hint of emotional involvement with him and Guy would be furious. Her

intense responses to his lovemaking were worrying enough as it was. Who knew how long she could successfully blame her reactions on her mysterious 'other lover'?

Thinking of that reminded her of the irony of what Guy had said during the aftermath of their lovemaking. His advice had been basically correct. The man she loved *was* stupid—in one regard—and she perhaps *shouldn't* be wasting her time on him. But it was very hard to have regrets when he had given her the most special night of her life, when he had made dreams come true, and when he had shown himself to be far more sensitive and considerate than she'd previously given him credit for.

He could have been blunt—or coarse—in their mating. Instead he had been imaginative and exciting and quite wonderful, not feeding her insecurities but flattering her and making her feel very special indeed. He didn't have to do that, but he had. The knowledge that the man she loved had a softer, more compassionate side pleased Samantha very much. It reassured her belief that he would be a good father. Thoughtful and loving, in the same manner that he was a thoughtful and loving son. It was only in forming deeper relationships with women that he was flawed.

She shook her head under the water with a black frustration. There were some women in this world—or perhaps not in this world!—who had a lot to answer for where Guy was concerned. His mother for one, she suspected, not to mention the three callous stepmothers who had flitted in and out of his young life, warping his youthful mind, turning him into an emotional cripple where male-female relationships were concerned.

Samantha eventually snapped off the water and dried herself with one of the lush blue towels. She had been right about the bathroom. It really did have everything that opened and shut, including a corner spa bath, tiled in royal blue with silver taps. There was even a small washer and tumble drier built into the wall behind the door, with concertina doors that could be closed in front of them to reduce the noise.

Samantha wrapped one of the enormous blue towels around herself, sarong-style, then hunted through the many and various drawers in the huge double bowl vanity in search of a hairbrush. She found a wide-toothed comb—blue, of course—and proceeded to make some order out of the knots and tangles of her thick brown hair.

One last look in the mirror showed a woman far removed from Miss Samantha Peters, prim and proper secretary. The faint smudges under her eyes from her slept-in mascara and the tellingly puffy lips conjured up the image of a mistress just tumbled from her lover's bed.

The thought sent a ripple of excitement and satisfaction through her. Guy was no longer just her boss. He was her lover!

But for how long, sweetheart? taunted that other brutally honest, more vulgar voice. A man as healthy and virile as Guy will hit a bull's-eye in no time flat! After that he won't come near you with a barge-pole, let alone...

'Shut up!' she spat as naked pain flashed into wounded hazel eyes. 'Shut up...'

Groaning, she swung away and with clenched fists strode over to the door, but as her hand lifted to turn the knob, her fingers extending, she could see it was shaking. Get a grip on yourself, girl! came the stern reprimand.

With stiff, jerky movements she wrenched open the door and walked into the bedroom, only to jolt to a halt. The bed—and the bedroom—was empty.

Startled, she hurried over to the double doorway that led into the sitting-room. That area too was empty.

Heat slammed into her cheeks as a quick glance around revealed nothing to disturb the room's serene blue tidiness but her own clothes scattered around: her blouse lying carelessly over the back of the sofa; her bra near the leg of a small table; the black culottes still pooled on the carpet.

And the red silk scarf where it had been thrown against a wall, the knot still in place.

Shock joined her embarrassment as she saw with more clarity what exactly she had allowed. Oh, God... How was she going to face him, calmly, dispassionately... after what she had let him do?

It was impossible! Certainly impossible as she was at that moment, still stark naked, but for a towel. One look at her would remind him. And herself. She couldn't bear to see any hint of male smugness in his face, any sort of triumph.

Sweeping up all the clothes, she raced back into the bedroom, where she reclaimed the rest from the foot of the bed. Fearing that Guy would walk back in at any moment, she fled into the bathroom and dressed in record time. The knot in the scarf, though, refused to budge to her fumbling, trembling fingers, and in the end she stuffed it into the small flip-top rubbish bin beside the vanity.

She actually managed to be sitting on one of the sofas, casually watching a Saturday morning music video show on television, when the door opened and Guy strode in.

The first thing she noticed was that he was both showered and as dressed as she was, in casual navy trousers and an open-necked pale blue shirt. The second thing that caught her eye was that he looked markedly strained.

Steely blue eyes flicked over her where she sat, nervously tongue-tied. 'I'm glad to see you're dressed,' he pronounced tautly. 'Would you like to have some breakfast here, or wait till you get home?'

Samantha stared at him as he strode over and picked up a set of keys from an ashtray on the bar. By the time he had shoved them into his trouser pocket and turned back to face her she had swallowed her shock and was able to look at him as indifferently as he was now looking at her.

'I'm going home, am I?' she asked with studied nonchalance, and levered herself to her feet. 'I wasn't sure what you had in mind. I thought you might want me to stay the whole weekend.'

A cold resolve settled in his eyes that might have sent a shiver down her spine if she hadn't already been frozen inside. Home... He was taking her home... He couldn't face making love to her again today...

'That *was* my original idea,' he admitted unexpectedly, 'but I wasn't prepared for what happened last night. I thought things would be... simpler. Under the circumstances, I think it best I take you home. I also think we should forget all about having a baby together at this point in time.'

'But——'

'It's quite clear to me,' he cut in sharply, 'that you're absolutely crazy about this other bloke, which means your decision-making processes have been affected. I don't need the mother of my child having some sort of nervous breakdown because of unrequited love.'

She was no longer able to hide her dismay. 'Yes, but...but I might already *be* pregnant,' she blurted out.

His face tightened. 'I doubt that very much. We'd have to be unlucky. But if it happens, it happens. We'll cross that bridge when we come to it. But as of now, Sam, I'm calling this whole project off!'

Dismay quickly gave way to a flare of anger. Who did he think he was, changing his mind like that, *now*? Couldn't he see he had no right to give her a glimpse of heaven then dash her back down to hell?

'Don't I have any say in the matter?'

Her cold fury surprised him, but he quickly gathered himself. 'No,' he returned curtly.

Her teeth clenched hard in her jaw. 'Just like that!' She snapped her fingers. 'You said we were partners in this, Guy. This doesn't sound to me as if we're partners. It sounds like a typical self-centred male boss telling his female employee what's going to be what, ordering her around as though she doesn't have any rights, or even brains!'

She lifted her chin in proud defiance. But her heart was racing and her mind searching desperately for the logic that would win for her a temporary extension of what had already become a dangerous addiction—Guy making love to her.

'Do you realise I find your decision insulting?' she argued, trying to sound as coldly reasoning as her desperation would allow. 'It assumes I'm wishy-washy and weak. Haven't you always said you liked my down-to-earth practicality, my common sense?

I thought you knew me better, Guy, than to judge me on a few female tears. We had a pact, you and I. A bargain! And now you're breaking it without good cause.'

'I do have good cause,' he stated in a low, controlled, but definitely angry voice.

'Oh, yes!' she flung back at him. 'This pathetic assumption that I might have a nervous breakdown.' Her laughter was bitter. 'Good God, if I was going to have a nervous breakdown it would have been while working for an impatient, intolerant, demanding bastard like you these past five years!'

His eyes flared wide with shock at her words.

Samantha turned to snatch up her handbag and stalked over to him. She stopped within arm's distance and glared up at him, blind anger making her careless. 'Has it ever occurred to you, Guy, that you might have made a few wrong deductions about last night? That things might not have been exactly as they seemed?'

Puzzlement leapt into his intelligent blue eyes. 'In what way?'

Only then did Samantha see the corner she had backed herself into. But, if there was one thing she had become adept at with having to handle Guy, it was the ability to think on her feet.

'I... I happen to like sex,' she came out with boldly. 'Very much. But because of this... this unrequited love of mine I haven't had any for ages. Last night I discovered I could still enjoy sex, despite that. My tears were tears of relief and gratitude, not misery. I was enjoying not some fantasy, but a real live man. *You*, Guy. I enjoyed *you*. Not someone else. And I think *you* enjoyed *me*. Oh, I know I'm not some fluffy little blonde with mincing ways and a sweet-as-apple-pie disposition, and I dare say your experience with me might not be the best you've ever had. But it was good, wasn't it?'

He straightened and glared down at her for a moment, then a black, sardonic smile creased his mouth. 'Yes,' he conceded drily. 'It was good.'

'Then why are you doing this?' she argued, emotion taking over again. 'Why? I...I don't understand you. We agreed. We talked about it. I...I want this baby, Guy. I want *your* baby,' she almost sobbed. 'Please, I...'

It was the worst thing she could have done; to betray such depth of emotion. He stared at her, a look of half-horror in his eyes as he visibly recoiled. Under her stricken gaze a stony mask dropped over his face and he took her arm in a harsh grip.

'I'm taking you home, Sam, and *don't* give me any arguments! Hell, if you've already fallen pregnant I'll...I'll... You can't have,' he muttered, throwing her a forbidding look as though he could stop such an event with his will alone. 'I worked it out. From my calculations, your most likely days are next Monday and Tuesday. Last night was supposed to be a damned dress rehearsal, a breaking of the ice, so to speak. What a laugh that is,' he mocked darkly. 'I find out my cool, conservative secretary is all fire, not ice. And *I*...' He made a scoffing sound and shook his head. 'I'm definitely not in the market for fiery secretaries. Or mothers!' And, closing his fingers tightly over her flesh, he shepherded her from the room.

Thankfully, they didn't encounter either Barbara or Leon in their hurried journey through the house to the garages. Samantha liked Guy's house-

keepers—and they liked her. God knew what they
would have made of the situation had they encountered her with him in so intimate a fashion.
Or would they be used, by now, to their employer
producing many and varied women the next
morning?

She didn't know. She didn't really care any more.
All she cared about was Guy, and he was taking
her home with a stern look on his face and determination in his heart never to have anything more
to do with her. No doubt he would let her work
out her four weeks—to fire her on the spot would
put him out—but she could imagine how strained
those weeks would be, especially the fortnight
leading up to her period.

Nevertheless, he was dead right about when her
most likely time to conceive was. She had worked
it out herself. She was due tomorrow evening fortnight, without fail, and the woman's book she kept
in a drawer beside her bed said twelve to fourteen
days before the first day was the peak time.
No...she wouldn't have fallen pregnant yet, she
thought bleakly as Guy bundled her into his car.
And now she never would.

The garage doors opened electronically, as did
his gates, Guy reversing out and getting under way
without having to leave his seat behind the wheel.
The clock fitted into the low-slung dashboard said
nine thirty-eight.

At precisely ten-fourteen Guy swung the silvery-
blue vehicle into the semicircular driveway in front
of her block of flats at Lane Cove. Not a word had
passed between them during the entire trip. Guy
had smoked non-stop, leading Samantha to think
bitterly that the sex had obviously not been *that*

good. A night with one of his blondes certainly cured him of the habit for a while.

'I'd rather you didn't come up,' she said tautly as she pushed open the door and unfolded herself from the passenger-seat.

Clearly Guy wasn't about to insist, since he hadn't alighted from behind the wheel. His face was the grimmest she had seen in many a month.

But then, her boss was not one who liked to make a mistake. Samantha could see that he would think he had erred drastically last night. He had made what he had considered a brilliant choice for the mother of his child, a woman of a similar cold mind to his, only to find out he'd been wrong.

'See you Monday morning,' she threw over her shoulder as she walked off, head held high.

The car growled behind her as it swung out of the driveway and leapt up the road.

Samantha would have liked to sink to the ground in a flood of tears. Instead she squared her shoulders and kept walking up the pathway that led into the building. As she approached the foyer area a movement overhead attracted her attention, and she looked up in time to see Tom crawling up the ivy on the wall to Lisa's balcony on the second floor. Unfortunately Lisa herself was leaning over the balcony railing, encouraging him, and from the look on her face she had witnessed Samantha's entire scene with Guy.

Just what I need, Samantha groaned, knowing the infernal girl would be down the stairs in a minute or two, pretending to be getting her washing but only wanting to probe for gossip.

Which was exactly what happened. No sooner had Samantha trudged up the stairs, let herself in and put the kettle on for a cup of tea than there was a knock on the door. With a resigned sigh she went to answer it. Lisa was standing there, smiling, waving a couple of letters. 'You forgot to bring in your mail yesterday,' she said, and held out the letters.

Samantha gave them both a brief glance. One was from her mother, the other from Aunt Vonnie. She drummed up a polite smile for her caller. 'Care to come in for a cuppa?'

'Don't mind if I do.' Lisa sashayed into the living-room, an attractive redhead in jeans and bright green jumper. She curled up in one of the two comfy armchairs. 'I came down earlier to get my washing, but you weren't in. Then when I went down to recover yesterday's mail from my box I saw you hadn't collected yours and I thought, that's strange. Samantha not getting her mail, then not coming home all night. Not like her at all. Then I saw you being deposited personally by the big man himself. That certainly raised my eyebrows, I can tell you. Care to tell me what gives? You and he got a thing going, have you?'

Any other time Samantha might have been able to come up with something to allay Lisa's curiosity, but she was flat out of façades and excuses. With a speed that stunned both of them she leant on the kitchen counter and burst into tears.

Lisa jumped to her feet, all initial fluster. But then she astounded Samantha with such genuine concern and warmth and sympathy that in no time Samantha was feeling awfully guilty for ever thinking the girl was anything less than a saint.

Lisa hugged her and soothed her, then took her by the shoulders and settled her gently on Samantha's flowered divan, got her tissues, patted her hand and insisted she stay put while she made the cup of tea, serving it with heaps of sugar in it. 'For shock,' she was told sweetly.

Samantha took tea without any sugar but didn't say a word, she was so overwhelmed by such a show of human kindness.

Never one to make close friends, she wasn't used to the way girlfriends, particularly, could generously support members of their own sex. In the next hour, however, she was to discover there was a whole world of affection and friendliness waiting out there, if only one would open oneself to it. She even found herself telling Lisa all about herself, and how she had been in love with her boss for years and, though she had resigned, she had last night finally gone to bed with him.

Of course she said nothing about her and Guy's now defunct plan to have a baby—that was too scandalous to voice aloud—letting the girl think that her upset was because, while the sex was good between them, her boss wanted to leave it with a one-night stand, so to speak, with no further involvement.

'What a bastard!' Lisa grimaced, curling her lip. 'Probably thought he'd have a bit, just because you're leaving, I'll bet. He didn't say he loved you, did he?'

'No!' Samantha defended, feeling guilty that Guy was being painted so black in Lisa's eyes. Though, damn it all, he was hardly lily-white!

'It's typical of those good-looking, successful bachelor types,' Lisa scorned. 'They always think all they have to do is snap their fingers and we girls will come across.' She dissolved into giggles at some private joke. 'The trouble is,' she spluttered, 'we usually do!'

Samantha found herself laughing with her. 'You're so right,' she agreed, grinning like a fool.

When they finally quietened Lisa gave her friend a more serious look. 'What are you going to do? Quit right now or go back for the final four weeks?'

Samantha dragged in a deep breath and expelled it wearily. 'I can't quit,' she said unhappily. 'I...it would let him down, and he's really not that bad. It's not as though he wasn't totally honest about last night. He...he doesn't know I love him either.'

'Huh! He still needs a good kick up the bum,' the girl grumbled. 'Still, I suppose, by staying, there's a better chance of his getting some come-uppance!'

'Come-uppance?' Samantha frowned.

'Sure thing. Tease the hell out of the devil. Give him some of his own medicine back!'

'But...but...'

'Come on, don't let the side down. We women have to fight back occasionally. He wouldn't have gone to bed with you even once if he didn't fancy you a bit, and, believe me, you could make him fancy you a whole lot more if you put your mind to it. Why should you be the only frustrated one? All you have to do is get rid of those ladylike suits you wear, don some sexier gear, slap on some brighter make-up and drown yourself in exotic perfume. Go for the jugular, honey. And I don't mean the one in his neck!'

Samantha was amazed by the girl's vehement and very down-to-earth words, but also undeniably stirred by them. She was right. By God, she was right! Why should she drift away like a wimp, take his rejection lying down? She'd give him a real eyeful over the next four weeks and, by golly, if he wasn't smoking like a bush campfire by the end of the month it wouldn't be for her want of trying.

Rebellious gleams flashed into her eyes and Lisa squealed with delight. 'You're going to, aren't you? Oh, goodie, goodie, goodie.' She jumped to her feet and clapped excitedly. 'Well, come on, come up to my flat and we'll play sexy dress-ups. I've got loads of outfits you can borrow till you can restock your wardrobe. There's this one dress...and on your body, honey, it'll knock your boss's eyes out!'

CHAPTER EIGHT

IT DIDN'T knock Guy's eyes out. Not literally.

But he certainly ground to a halt when Samantha stood up casually and offered to get him a cup of coffee the moment he walked in on the Monday morning. Her upstanding position gave him a clear view of the way the red wool crêpe dress transformed her figure into an hourglass, a wide self-covered belt cinching her tightly in at the waist, making her full bust and curvy hips even more pronounced.

Lisa had said that, even on her own more slender body, the red dress had drawn a lot of male stares.

'On your figure, honey,' she'd drawled, 'it would rejuvenate a jaundiced octogenarian with arthritis and a squint.'

It certainly was drawing Guy's attention—or perhaps it was her loosely flowing hair or extra make-up that he was staring at. Whatever, he did his best to cover any sexual interest by adopting one of his bland business faces, complete with feigned indifference. And it *was* feigned. Samantha had seen the brief but definite flash of desire in his eyes when they'd clamped on the thrust of her breasts as she rose. Now, as he walked on, she detected a clenching of the muscles along his jawline.

'No, thanks,' he said with telling sharpness. 'I'll make my own when I'm ready.'

A weird sense of triumph rippled through Samantha as she stood there and watched his dis-

comfort. Lisa had been right. He did fancy her.
How could he not after what they had shared? Guy
was very much a lover of female flesh, the epitome
of male virility. Once having been made aware of
a woman sexually—even if by unusual cir-
cumstance—he wouldn't be able to switch off that
awareness so easily. Especially if visually reminded
of it.

He strode over to drop his briefcase down beside
his desk, then returned to stand in the doorway,
looking at her. No desire now, only a faint sardonic
derision.

'Going to a party after work?' he said mockingly.

Samantha had anticipated he would question her
changed appearance, and was glad she had a ready-
made excuse. It wasn't even a lie, either. During
her dressing-up session with Lisa she'd finally read
the letters Lisa had collected for her. Aunt Vonnie's
contained nothing out of the ordinary but her
mother's had supplied the rather unnerving news
that her old friend Norman was coming to Sydney
for a few days and wanted to see her.

Thank heaven her mother had thought not to give
him her home address. She had, however, supplied
Norman with the phone number and address of
Haywood Promotions and, since he'd been due to
arrive some time over the weekend and was staying
at an inner-city hotel, it was highly likely he would
drop by either today or tomorrow. At the time of
the news Samantha had cringed away from seeing
Norman again. Now it gave her a certain amount
of pleasure to be able to throw the possibility of
another man's interest in Guy's face.

'Well?' Guy went on, more testily this time. 'Are
you or are you not going out after work? There has

to be some reason for this.' He waved a dismissive hand in the direction of the red dress.

Samantha looked boldly back at him and tried to ignore *his* body, resplendently housed in a pale grey three-piece suit that had a slight sheen to it, and accessories that would have put a dent in most people's weekly pay-packet: white silk shirt, black and grey striped tie, black leather shoes. His dark hair was slicked back from his handsome face in that way that suggested he had not long been in his shower.

Unfortunately, thoughts of showers brought other disturbing images. It irritated Samantha that she had vowed to disturb *him*, not the other way around. Pique had her dampening her hot thoughts behind a hardening heart.

'No,' she stated brusquely. 'A friend might be taking me out to lunch.'

'Really? Anyone I know?'

Samantha was startled by the vibrating tension in Guy's voice. He began walking slowly towards her.

'No, I wouldn't think so,' she said, whirling away to hurry into the kitchenette, forgetting momentarily about the back of her dress. But she quickly remembered when cool air whooshed in the slit that ran from the back of her neck to the waist.

'Would you be cold in that dress?' Guy asked drily as he followed her into the kitchenette.

Battling a fierce blush and a sharp loss of confidence—this type of garment was really not her style—Samantha gave a brilliantly offhand shrug. 'Most places are air-conditioned these days, and I have a jacket.' She nodded towards the black crêpe blazer that completed the outfit and was hanging on the coat-rack beside the small refrigerator.

She could feel him behind her, staring at the strip of bare flesh. 'Is this old friend the man you love?' he asked at last in a low, taut voice.

She turned slowly and was taken aback by the glittering anger in his eyes. 'No,' she replied evenly. 'Anyway, why should you care if it *were*?'

For a second she thought he was going to slap her. Yet he didn't lift a finger. But something flashed in his eyes that was swift and violent and quite frightening, and she had difficulty stopping herself from visibly flinching away.

'I'm merely checking,' he ground out, 'that you don't have sex with anyone else till we know if you're pregnant or not. I have no intention of financially supporting some other man's child.'

So that was it, she thought with a bitter despair. Not jealousy. Or sexual possessiveness. Merely a protecting of his male pride and his precious bank balance. Oh, Lisa, Lisa, you don't know this man. He's not your everyday fool. He can't be manipulated that easily. Heavens, he can get his sex wherever he wants and from women he infinitely prefers to me!

Something shrivelled inside her with this acceptance, and she felt totally stupid and embarrassed in the dress. Her own pride, however, kept her outer shell erect, her eyes steady, her chin up. 'I am not promiscuous, Guy, if that's what you're implying. I never have been and I never will be.'

'Really? Well, answer me this, my suddenly sexy secretary. This old friend of yours. Have you ever been to bed with him?'

God, but she tried hard not to colour. Damnably hard. But she was doomed to failure.

As guilty heat flooded her face Guy's reaction was quite astonishing. His face darkened also, a slash of red across his cheeks. She could have sworn he was jealous now. Jealous and angry. But in the end she conceded that it was probably only fury at having to accept she had seemingly fooled him about her character. Without saying a word, he spun away and stormed off into his office, slamming the door behind him.

Samantha let out a shuddering sigh. She felt confused and terribly unhappy at the incident. The only thing she could be certain of any more was that in just under four weeks she would leave here with head held high, for there would be no more red dresses, no more pathetic attempts at sexual teasing, no more humiliation. If she didn't have her own self-respect, she had nothing!

The morning dragged by, an eternity of small hells, for it seemed that was the day everyone and anyone chose to drop in and see Guy. And, consequently, the red dress!

Most made no direct comment, merely raised eyebrows and gave curious looks, but shortly before noon Frankie appeared, flushed with his recent success.

'Hi, doll-face. The boss in?' he quipped as he marched in, flinging the door shut behind him. Frankie never walked. He marched. Suddenly his eyes snapped round to stare at her loose hair, then lower. 'Wow! What have you done to yourself? My God, I won't be able to keep my hands off you if you go around looking like that. Hell, put me in solitary confinement! Throw me in the stockade! Lash me to the mast!'

'Aren't you mixing your metaphors, Frankie?' Guy said in dry amusement as he came through his door and pumped his favourite client's hand in greeting. 'Lashing to the mast is a naval expression.'

'Navel!' Frankie groaned and put the back of his left hand to his forehead in mock distress. 'Don't start talking about bare flesh or I'll faint with desire. How do you stand it, dear friend, having this vision of loveliness at your beck and call?'

'With great difficulty,' Guy intoned flatly, and threw Samantha a black look. She cringed inside, especially at the dark fluttering that crept into her stomach with his derisive glance. Even when despising her, he could still affect her sexually, she realised. It was mortifying in the extreme.

She was infinitely relieved when Guy drew Frankie into the inner sanctum, saying he had new material to discuss with him for his television spot. It was as she was relishing the respite from tension that Lisa rang.

'How's it going?' was her first question. 'Is he squirming yet?'

'I'll tell you who's squirming,' Samantha confessed unhappily. '*Me*. Truly, Lisa, I appreciate the loan of the dress and everything, but I can't handle it. Everyone's been staring at me as if I've just landed from Mars—that is, the ones who aren't making openly lustful remarks. As for Guy... He's been looking at me as if he's just discovered I'm a call-girl—with potential diseases to boot!'

'Oh, sure! I'll bet he's just acting. I'll bet underneath it all he's suffering like hell,' the other girl scoffed.

'What if he is? He'll just go out and get himself another woman, not me.'

Lisa sighed. 'I guess so. Gee, what a shame. I thought he'd be so turned on by your stunning figure on display that he'd sweep you into his office and take you on the desk.'

'*Lisa!*'

'Only a figure of speech, dearie. Of course, you would show some resistance, then melt at the appropriate moment. Oh, well... "The best-laid schemes o' mice an' men..."'

'Do... do you really think I've got a stunning figure?' Samantha asked hesitantly. Having once been overweight and the butt of jokes, she found it hard to believe the evidence of her own mirror. Though she knew she had enviable breasts, she had always thought her hips and bottom were too curvy, and that she was too tall.

Lisa sighed impatiently. 'Whatever am I going to do with you? Of course you've got a stunning figure. Mind-blowing! No red-blooded man could resist it. Oh, yes, I know, you told me all about those little blonde dolly-birds your boss seems to like. But that's not *your* fault. The man's obviously got a problem. Maybe he's afraid to grow up emotionally, to have a woman in his life he might actually want to commit to, one with some real beauty and brains.'

'You think so?'

'I'd bet my drinking money on it.'

Samantha fell silent. There could be something in what Lisa had said, about Guy resisting emotional maturity. Perhaps, Samantha mused, it was because he had never had a role model in his life to copy. She had been blaming his mother and stepmothers for his emotional flaws, when perhaps she should have been looking at his father.

Martin Haywood, the charming rogue who'd consistently failed in marriage and maybe countless other relationships. Was it because he'd been unlucky in his choices of women? Or because he had deliberately made those choices, deliberately picked the sort of superficial sexy female who was great in bed for a while, but impossible for a man of intelligence to really love?

Possibilities and probabilities whirled in her mind. But then she sighed, for what would a successful analysis of Guy's behaviour prove anyway? Only that he was screwed up and she shouldn't be getting mixed up with him, that in the end he would hurt her, even if she did succeed in getting into his bed again, even if she talked him back into having a baby together.

No, she conceded bleakly. That last idea was definitely gone. He wouldn't come at that again. There was never going to be a little boy or girl for her to love, no bond to keep this man—however tenuously—by her side forever.

'Samantha?' came the soft enquiry. 'Are you all right?'

A lump formed in her throat. 'Yes.'

'I'll drop down and see you this evening, make sure.'

'You're...very kind.'

'You're a nice person.'

'So are you,' she choked out, and said a quick goodbye before she burst into tears on the girl again.

She was hanging up the receiver when there was a tentative knock on the office door. Somehow she knew it was Norman even before she opened it. Tentative, shy little Norman. But, dear heaven, she really wasn't in the mood for a reunion.

She opened the door with a rueful resignation, only to find her neck stretching upwards and her lips falling apart in startled surprise. Oh, yes, it was Norman, all right, but when had he shot up to this height, found this amazing width? And where, she finally registered, had all his pimples gone to?

Fortunately, he was looking at her with equal astonishment and hardly noticed hers, his brown eyes raking over her body with definite appreciation. 'I know that's you, Amazon Sam,' he teased gently, 'because you've the same lovely hair and eyes. But what happened to the rest of you?'

'I think *you've* got it all,' she laughed. 'Oh, Norman, it's so good to see you.' And, suddenly, it was!

'And you too. Have you got a kiss for your old school-mate?'

The old Norman would have stood tremulously waiting for her to give permission. This Norman pulled her into a bear-hug and planted a kiss on her lips that wasn't too presumptuous, but could hardly be called platonic. By the time he let her go she felt as if she'd been run over by a bulldozer.

'Your lunch date, I presume?' Guy said coldly from just behind her.

Norman swung her round half behind him, stepping forward to take Guy's hand in his large grip. 'You'd be Samantha's boss, I guess. Look, I've got a favour to ask, mate. I'm only going to be in town a few days and I'm lined up to visit relatives from tomorrow on. Do you think you could give my girl the afternoon off? I haven't seen her in donkey's ages and we've got a lot of catching up to do, haven't we?' This with a wide smile her way.

'I'm sorry,' Guy returned curtly, 'but I'll need Samantha back here this afternoon. I...'

'Don't be such a party-pooper, Guy,' Frankie joined in, coming forward with a big grin on his face. 'You'll survive without Sam for one miserable afternoon.'

Cold blue eyes settled on her. 'You think so?' he drawled.

'Yeah. Go on, doll-face. Get going with your date while I lash the boss here to the mast!' He laughed at his own joke. 'Of course, you'll have to work on late tomorrow night to make up for it, won't she, Guy?' he finished with a sly dig in his ribs.

'Indubitably.'

'I'll just get my jacket,' Samantha said with a reprimanding look at both Frankie and Guy. She hoped Norman was still country enough not to understand their underlying crudities.

But as he walked her down the corridor towards the lift he darted her a long, thoughtful glance and said, 'Well, Samantha? And just how long have you been sleeping with your boss?'

CHAPTER NINE

IT TOOK every ounce of Samantha's acting ability and an entire hour over coffee and sandwiches to convince Norman he had jumped to the wrong conclusion, and that these sexual *double entendres* were a type of teasing, common in any workplace in the city.

And of course he basically *was* wrong. She had not 'been sleeping' with Guy. She had slept with him *once*, and was unlikely ever to do so again.

So she joked and laughed over his accusation, taking the sting out of her own shock that Norman was no man's fool these days. It was a relief too to find out that he was about to become safely engaged to a nice girl back home and had decided to see Samantha on his trip to Sydney more to lay an old ghost to rest, rather than to try to revive ancient history.

After that both of them relaxed, and the hours they spent together were very enjoyable indeed. Samantha showed Norman the best tourist spots in the city, the shops and beauty of the Queen Victoria Building, Darling Harbour, the Rocks, the bridge, the opera house, the botanical gardens. By the time he took her back to his city hotel for an evening meal they were both a fraction foot-worn, but very much at ease in each other's company.

Yes, they spent a very pleasant time together.

Nevertheless, when Norman walked her through the hotel foyer on his way to putting her in a taxi he stopped briefly and placed a caring hand on her arm. 'Be careful, Samantha,' he warned gently. 'I know what you said about your relationship with your boss, but I can't help thinking there *is* something between you, something...simmering. You're not in his league, love. You're country, no matter what you may look like now. He's city. From what I gather, city men play hard and fast with women. I'd give him a wide berth if I were you.'

Samantha covered his hand with one of her own and smiled softly. 'You don't have to worry about me, Norman. I'm leaving my present job in a few weeks. I might even come home for a while.'

This brought a flash of panic into his eyes. 'God, don't do that! Raeleen will have a pink fit when she sees you. She's jealous of you enough as it is.'

Samantha was taken aback. 'But... but why?'

Norman looked sheepish. 'I made the mistake of telling her about you when we first went out. She wanted to know who...you know... I'm afraid I must have raved about you a bit. She accused me of still being in love with you. I—er—I soothed her jealousy by saying you were...um...rather plain and plump.'

'Oh...I see... But don't worry, Norman. I don't usually look like this. I *can* look quite ordinary, believe me.'

His face was decidedly sceptical.

Samantha gave him another soothing smile and patted his hand. 'Don't worry. If I come home it'll only be for a flying visit. I'm off up to Brisbane,' she improvised. 'Your Raeleen won't even know I've been there if you don't tell her. I'm not likely to come out to your farm, am I?'

Norman was still looking slightly worried as he helped her into the back of the taxi. 'It was lovely seeing you again, Norman,' she said, and lifted her mouth for a goodnight kiss. It amused her that he made it a very curt peck, as though Raeleen could somehow see what he was doing. Maybe he was thinking ahead, of the third degree his girlfriend would give him when he got home.

Aah, jealousy, she mused. And immediately thought of Guy. Had he been jealous of her going out with someone else? Norman had apparently thought so. Or was Guy just still concerned that she might go to bed with another man then try to pin the pregnancy on him? Yes, she thought ruefully. That sounded more like it.

It made her sad to think that he didn't know her at all really, that he was actually getting a very warped idea of her character in all this.

But what could she do about it? Tell him the whole truth and nothing but the truth? What would that achieve, except embarrassment for both of them? No... She would just have to endure the next few weeks, then get the hell out of his life. Maybe Brisbane was not such a bad idea...

The light was still on in Lisa's flat when she got home, so she went up and knocked on the door. 'It's only me,' she called out.

Lisa wrenched open the door, a real sight with a face mask on and her hair bundled up in a shower cap.

'Goodness,' Samantha chuckled, 'aren't we glamorous this evening?'

The other girl ushered her in with curious eagerness. 'Does the late hour and your good humour mean success came late in the day? Did gorgeous Guy finally capitulate and ravish you in the office then take you out for wining and dining?'

Samantha plopped down in a chair with a sigh. 'Sorry. No success in that department. But I *have* spent a pleasant evening with a very old schoolfriend, come to the big smoke for a holiday. Actually, he was my first—er—you know.'

'*No*! You mean one of those country yokels out in woop-woop did the dastardly deed?' Lisa was all ears. 'Tell me all the gory details. Where? When? *How*?'

Samantha reluctantly satisfied her friend's avid curiosity, then rose, yawning. 'Must go to bed. I have the feeling Guy will be like a bear with a sore head tomorrow and work the pants off me. Oh! I mean...'

For a second she looked horrified, then both of them dissolved into helpless giggles. Despite her deep-down misery, Samantha left the flat smiling. Truly, that girl was corrupting her!

Samantha was right, though, about Guy the next day. He made a bear with a sore head seem goodtempered. Even her return to conservative dressing made no difference, her hair up and subdued choice of plain black suit and businesslike white blouse bringing a sour look when he arrived shortly after nine. Surprisingly early for him.

'I take it you haven't any lunch dates today?' he flung at her caustically as he strode past her desk, his own subdued dark suit not doing enough to hide *his* sex appeal, Samantha thought bitterly.

'Not that I know of,' she tossed back with superb coolness.

This brought another sharp look, after which he hibernated in his office for half an hour—most of which he spent on the phone—before coming out, snapping demands, from wanting a list of every music video director and photographer in Australia to having her find out the address and phone number of some obscure songwriter whose name was very inconveniently James Smith.

She smiled her compliance through gritted teeth, printing the first list from her database on her computer quite easily, but sighing frustratedly as she began ringing every J. Smith in the Sydney phone directory. By a stroke of luck, however, the songwriter was in the first half-dozen names and it gave her some malicious satisfaction to be able to swan into Guy's office and give him what he wanted within minutes.

He glared up at her in disbelief. 'Do you have a genie in your drawer?' he snarled.

'No. A computer on my desk,' she returned calmly, and began to make a totally unruffled exit.

'Sam!' he called, halting her as she reached the door.

She turned slowly. 'What?'

He was looking at her quite strangely, with an odd bleakness in his eyes. 'I suppose your resignation still stands.'

Her mouth tightened so that it wouldn't tremble. 'What do *you* think?' The effort to control the stab of dismay brought a sharp edge to her voice and words.

'I think no one,' he said softly, 'will ever be able to take your place.'

Her heart turned over and at that moment she hated him, hated him for trying to sway her with emotional blackmail. 'I doubt that very much,' she bit out. 'No one's indispensable, certainly not around you! If you'll excuse me, I think Mrs Walton has just come in.'

She *had*, thank the lord, which was a good defence for the next four hours. By the time the other woman left Samantha felt totally drained from pretending everything was fine.

She glanced up at the clock. After two already... and she still hadn't had any proper lunch. Guy had stalked out of the office at one, leaving a whole pile of typing for her to do, compiling jokes from various comedy books and magazines he had underlined—obviously for Frankie. Some of them were very funny, but she didn't feel like laughing.

Crying was closer to the mark.

She had just finished when Guy walked back in at two twenty-five, looking decidedly less strained. Perhaps all he'd needed was a good feed. Or maybe he'd spent his lunch-hour with a handy blonde, she thought caustically.

'Mrs Walton gone?' he asked.

'Yes. Here's that typing you wanted.' She handed him the printed pages without looking at him. 'I'm going to get a bite to eat myself. If you'll excuse me...' She got up and retreated to the safety of the wash-room.

After a quick tidy-up she emerged totally composed, and was about to pick up her handbag and leave when Guy called her into his office.

'Yes?' she said, staying near the open doorway.

He glanced up from his desk, blue eyes penetrating. They raked over her and she could see his mind ticking over as it did when he was assessing a difficult business colleague he needed something from, but whom he didn't want to ask. He reached for and lit a fresh cigarette, even though there was a butt still smouldering in his ashtray, the action forcing Samantha to accept she'd been wrong about his being more relaxed. It had been another façade, like the one she was exercising on herself at this moment.

His eyes returned to her through the puff of smoke, disturbing her with the quality of stubborn resolve that slid slowly into them.

'Have dinner with me tonight,' he said quietly.

For a second Samantha was so astonished that she could think of no reply. Then the penny dropped. He was still going to try to talk her out of leaving. After all that had happened. There could be no other explanation.

'You're wasting your time, Guy,' she said coldly. 'I'm leaving and that's that. Besides, I have plans for tonight.' Writing her weekly letters to her parents and Aunt Vonnie, then washing her hair. Very exciting stuff.

His eyes flashed with instant anger but he controlled it well. Clearly he felt only a calm approach would win him what he wanted.

'Another date with your old flame?'

'No.'

'Surely not a *new* one? For a girl who's supposed to have a broken heart, you're mighty resilient.'

Samantha stifled her growing fury. It's not all his fault, she thought with bitter honesty. I've fed him a lot of twisted truths, and now they're rebounding on me. There's no escape either. I have no option but to keep following the same, ghastly path.

Calmly, though, she told herself. Calmly...

'I have no date at all. I have things to do. My life doesn't begin and end with Haywood Promotions, you know.'

Goodness, was that *her*, using that icy, reprimanding voice?

'As for my heart, Guy,' she went on, just as chillingly, 'believe me, it's still well and truly broken. I just don't choose to wear it on my sleeve.'

She saw his blue eyes harden in retaliation, saw the muscles in his jaw twitch with suppressed irritation. 'Good for you, Sam. Still...you must understand my concern about your...*activities* till your next period. You're not quite the wallflower you always pretended to be.'

'It's amazing,' she snapped, 'how people judge others by their own morals. Believe it or not, dear Guy, I *am* capable of going out with a man and not leaping into bed with him. I do see more in the opposite sex than just the physical. Neither do I need a new face on the pillow practically every time I turn over.'

She glared at him and he stared back, clearly surprised by her attack.

'Is that what you think I am?' he said, startled. 'A compulsive womaniser?'

'*Aren't* you?'

He frowned then shrugged. 'Perhaps. In some people's eyes.' His frown cleared to a cynical amusement, his sigh carrying a strange satisfaction. 'So... Lover-boy from the bush didn't talk you back to his hotel room, after all.'

'No, he didn't,' she said irritably. 'And, for your information, Norman was never my *lover*. We did have sex together once, on our graduation night eight years ago when we were silly adolescents. Norman because he was a typical randy teenage boy, and me because I thought he needed me. I didn't even enjoy it. I do silly things like that sometimes. I guess I'm a sucker for people in need!'

'That's good, then,' Guy pronounced, and got to his feet.

Samantha's chest constricted as he started coming towards her, his steps purposeful and determined, decidedly passionate lights glittering in his eyes.

'Because I'm in need, Sam,' he said in a low, seductive voice. 'I'm definitely in need...'

She felt mesmerised, like a rabbit caught in the headlights of a car, standing there staring at him, unable to move or say anything. He came up to her and curled surprisingly gentle hands over her shoulders, easing her startled body over and back against the wall next to the door.

His first kisses were soft and patient, teasing her lips open, waiting for the groan that finally fluttered from her throat. Then his hands lifted to her face and he was holding her captive for the velvet heat of his tongue as it plundered her mouth, over and over. She was gasping by the time his lips slid across to an ear then down her throbbing throat, his impassioned words sending tremors of desire richocheting throughout her body.

'Sweet Sam... Sexy Sam... Did I ever know you...? I don't think so... But I want you... God, I want you... Don't deny me... Here...let me...' Shaking hands were under her jacket, on her blouse, reefing it out of the waistband. Then they were on bare flesh, around her back, fumbling to unhook her bra, making her heart race madly as she felt her breasts fall heavy and naked into his hungry hands. Thumbs rubbed over already hard nipples, his mouth seeking hers again, his tongue darting forward.

It was only when she felt cooler air on her thighs that she realised his hands had left her breasts to begin lifting her straight skirt upwards. An insistent male leg was prising her thighs apart.

'No, you can't!' she cried, gasping away from the imprisoning pressure of his mouth. 'Not here... Someone might come in...'

One foot reached out and kicked the door shut, one hand leaving her skirt momentarily to turn the lock.

Samantha's stomach flipped over with recognition of what he was about to do, and Lisa's teasing words catapulted back into her mind—'...he'd be so turned on he'd...take you on the desk.'

She had been shocked then. She was shocked now. But not for the same reason. Her present shock was all directed at herself, at the wave of sweet and utter surrender flooding up through her body. Wall...floor...desk... It no longer mattered. There was no question of stopping him. No question at all.

'Yes...yes,' she moaned when his fingers found and started stroking the satiny flesh between her thighs.

Her utter abandon must have startled him, for his head jerked up and he looked stunned as he stared down at her glazed eyes.

But she was beyond shame. 'I want you,' she whispered huskily. 'Don't you know that? Ever since last Friday night I've been wanting you...'

Her words had the opposite effect of what she wanted. He stopped. 'You deliberately teased me in that dress yesterday, didn't you?' he asked, eyes flaring angrily as his hands curled over her shoulder, fingers biting deep into her flesh. '*Didn't you*?' he repeated, shaking her.

'Yes.'

'You bitch,' he groaned, and swept her up into his arms, carrying her over to the chesterfield. There he laid her down and slowly undressed her, till she was all burning nakedness against the chill of the leather. His eyes remained angry as he bent his mouth to her, deliberately driving her to the jagged, panting edge of release before leaving her to begin taking off his own clothes. He took his time, watching her all the while with hooded, smouldering eyes, enjoying her frustration.

'You will never do such a thing to me again, Samantha Peters,' he grated out as he returned to take a rough possession of her still pulsating flesh. 'Never,' he repeated, and began to surge into her, deeply, passionately.

Samantha's body immediately splintered into sharp, convulsive spasms, but Guy seemed oblivious of her climax, his mad mating continuing, each thrust punctuated with wild words. 'Because I mean to have you...every time I want you...wherever I want you...however I want you...I will have you...and have you...till I drive these demons away...till I——'

His voice was choked off by a guttural cry, his whole body trembling uncontrollably as he began to shudder into her. Finally he slumped forward across her, his chest still heaving, raw gasps bursting from his lungs. Samantha gathered him in, stroking his sweat-covered back, gentling him with tender, loving words of bitter-sweet submission. 'Yes, yes,' she murmured, and kissed his shoulder, his chest, his neck. 'I'm yours...for as long as you want me...'

Dismay claimed her heart as the import of her own words sank in. For they encapsulated the only sort of relationship Guy could make with a woman, that of temporary lover. Sooner or later, when his passion had finally been sated, when sexual boredom set in, she would be discarded as every other woman in his life had been discarded. It might be three months from now, maybe four, definitely by six. Six months had always been his limit.

And it was while she was accepting these bleak thoughts that she remembered about the baby.

'Oh, my God!' She jerked up under him, pushing him away from her so that she could sit up.

'What the...?' He stared at her through glazed, smoky eyes.

'It's Tuesday!' she groaned.

The appalled horror that catapulted into his eyes was unmistakable. Quite clearly he too had forgotten. And, even more clearly, he no longer wanted her to fall pregnant, to have his baby. He now wanted something entirely different from her.

Samantha's emotions were torn in two. How ironic, she thought, that she had achieved one part of what she wanted—Guy's sexual desire—only to lose something else: his previously fervent wish for her to be the mother of his child.

'So it is,' he said, with bitter regret in his voice. 'So it is...' And he swung his feet over the side of the chesterfield, scooping his hair back from his forehead in a frustrated gesture.

Her eyes darted over at him, and for a second she felt a different pain, a panic. Surely he wouldn't ask her to have an abortion if she had conceived? Surely not? 'Guy,' she said, her heart fluttering wildly. 'There's no need to be upset. It's...it's what we originally planned, isn't it?'

He gave a dry laugh as he slanted her a hard look. 'Our original plan had certain prerequisites. Things have undergone some changes around here.'

'In...what way do you mean?' she asked. Was he talking about her character? Or the changing face of their relationship? His sudden and unexpected passion for her?

He stood up and started to drag on his clothes. Samantha watched him for a moment, then, feeling suddenly embarrassed, she got to her feet and began to do likewise.

'I didn't expect us to be so... physically in tune,' he said curtly. 'It presents... a problem.'

'Why?'

He threw her an exasperated look. 'For pity's sake, Sam, you must realise that once a man and woman become sexually besotted with each other there's a danger of further emotional involvement creeping in. One of them might think they've fallen in love and then there's hell to pay. Hell,' he repeated darkly, and expelled a shuddering sigh. 'Still...' he flashed her a worried look '...I guess, since you're in love with some other man, then things mightn't get out of hand. And, dammit, I *do* want our child, regardless...'

He was frowning grimly but Samantha hadn't heard a thing past his first sentence. 'Are you really sexually besotted with me, Guy?' she asked breathlessly.

His mouth curved into an ironic smile, his hand stilling on the belt of his trousers. 'Do you want further proof?'

Her own hands froze on the buttons of her blouse, her first instinct to drop her eyes modestly and say no. But something had been swept aside in Samantha that afternoon, *Guy* had swept it aside with his blistering passion, his no-holds-barred lovemaking. Any natural coyness and shyness seemed no longer relevant. She faced him with total sexual honesty. 'Yes,' she said.

It took his breath away. Literally.

But then he smiled again, and she knew he was still way ahead of her in that department. His hand reached out to trace her stiff puffy lips, to brush over her nipples through her clothes. She quivered under his touch.

'How have you hidden this side of yourself from me for so long?' he said thickly, his eyes narrowed with desire.

She shook her head, her tongue thick in her mouth, her throat dry.

His laugh was soft as he moved to draw her into his arms. 'I presume you didn't bring your overnight bag with you to the office today?' he murmured.

Again she shook her head.

He sighed in mock disappointment. 'You'll have to sleep in my bed tonight in the altogether, then, won't you?'

Another little shiver ran through her.

'But first things first.' His lips curved back into a wry smile as he started undressing her again. 'The things we men have to suffer to have a child...'

CHAPTER TEN

BY THE following morning there was no going back for Samantha, in any sense of the word. Guy wanted her as much as she wanted him. And, while common sense told her that one day her happiness would end, that infernal optimist named hope kept telling her Guy might change this time. This time, if she had his baby, his emotions could become engaged too and he might fall in love with her.

It was possible. *Anything* was possible, she decided. Look what had happened already. A few days ago she would never have believed she would become Guy's mistress, that he would look at her with such passion, such desire. Even after he had finished making love to her last night for the umpteenth time, he had seemed to still want her, touching her all the time, giving her the most seductive compliments. What woman wouldn't melt when told repeatedly she was the sexiest, most desirable woman in the world? What woman wouldn't respond by trying to make the words come true, by giving herself totally to such a lover, without inhibition, without shame?

The next two weeks passed for Samantha on a high plateau of sexual awareness and arousal, which perhaps transmitted itself to the man she loved, for Guy could not seem to get enough of her. Morning, noon and night he wanted to make love. No place was sacrosanct, no time.

Once, when Mrs Walton had been in the office longer than usual, Guy sent the poor woman out on an errand clear across the city. Even so, they were scarcely dressed when she returned, and later that night, when they were locked in each other's arms in Guy's bed, he suggested naughtily she wear wider skirts and less underwear to the office in future.

The Samantha of a couple of weeks ago would never have dreamt of being so daring. But there was no embarrassment or resistance in her relationship with Guy, only eager willingness to please, so intense were her feelings for him.

Besides, after that first time in the office he was never cruel to her, never at all crude. He suggested, never demanded. Persuaded, never took. Seduced, never forced.

He was also incredibly loving, always making her feel cherished afterwards, never used. Oh, yes, he could be wildly passionate, once he had secured her co-operation. Then he would lose control entirely, but he always held her tenderly during the aftermath of their torrid lovemaking, talking softly to her, as if she was a fragile, precious thing that he valued above all else.

No wonder all those other women were crazy about him, she thought occasionally with bitter jealousy. But then she would put those thoughts out of her head and try to enjoy each wonderful moment they shared.

She was pleased too that Guy didn't attempt to hide her overnight stays at his home, proudly taking her down to breakfast the next morning. Despite an initial surprise, Barbara and Leon soon got used to her new role in Guy's life, Barbara even going so far as to make some not so subtle remarks about 'some men taking years to grow up in their choice of women, but when they did they surpassed themselves'.

Mrs Walton, however, was kept blissfully in the dark. A dear woman, she was inclined to be a fraction strait-laced.

Lisa, of course, was very pleased for her friend, though not so pleased about not seeing Samantha so often for a cuppa and a chat.

'I'm lucky to catch you in these days,' Lisa complained at the communal laundry one Sunday. By this time Samantha's period was three weeks late and she was pretty sure she was pregnant. But Guy had insisted over the weekend that she go to the doctor for confirmation, so she'd made an appointment for first thing on the Monday morning at her local medical centre.

'Had to come home to do some washing,' she laughed.

'The boss still keeping you happy, I see,' Lisa winked. 'Any talk of marriage?'

Samantha's heart squeezed a little. 'No. He's not the marrying kind. I told you.'

Lisa shrugged. 'Men are always not the marrying kind. Till they meet the right girl.'

'Not Guy,' Samantha said. 'He's a confirmed bachelor.'

'Then what on earth are you bothering with him for?' Lisa asked bluntly. 'You don't seem the type of girl who would settle for an affair.'

The remark brought Samantha up with a jolt. How was she ever going to explain to people like Lisa about the baby, except by making it look like a mistake? Suddenly she realised she didn't want that. Not at all.

'The truth is, Lisa,' she said carefully, 'I have a secondary reason for having an affair with Guy. He...he told me one day that, even though he's not into marriage, he wanted a child to love, and so——'

'And so you offered your services,' Lisa cut in drily.

'Well, yes...'

Lisa was shaking her head. 'Oh, dear, oh, dear, oh, dear. Noble sacrifice is always a big mistake, love. Still...I can appreciate your dilemma. Hard to pass up all that sex with the man you love. Not to mention the little bit of him you get to keep forever. OK,' she sighed resignedly, 'when's the babe due? Do you want me to knit blue or pink or a neutral colour?'

Samantha gave an embarrassed laugh. 'How do you know I'm even pregnant yet?'

'Oh, honey... One look at that virile boss of yours and *I'm* nearly pregnant. After all these weeks of your tippy-toeing home at all hours, if at all, you're sure to be in the club.'

Samantha started to laugh outright. Lisa was always so good for her morale.

But she went to bed that night, quite keyed up over her doctor's appointment the following morning. What if she *wasn't* pregnant? What if she was just late?

Ten a.m. the next day found her hurrying along the corridor towards the office, the doctor's words still ringing in her ears. 'Yes, Miss Peters, the test's positive. From your dates, the baby's due mid-February...'

She felt hopelessly excited. She was definitely going to have a baby. A real baby. Right at this very moment a tiny little human being was actually growing inside her.

Goodness, Samantha realised, her face aglow with happiness. I'm going to be a *mother*!

She stopped before she reached the office door and ran a trembling hand over her stomach.

'Can you hear me, my child?' she whispered. 'I'm your mother. I wonder...will you call me Mum, or Mummy? Will you be blue-eyed, like your daddy, or hazel, like me? And will you love me as much as I know I'm going to love you, sweet precious darling?'

Samantha sighed happily, then hurried on, opening the office door and walking in with a silly grin on her face, only to find the office had a visitor. Guy's father was sitting in her chair and Guy was perched on the edge of the desk, both looking decidedly grim.

'Oh!' she exclaimed, taken aback. She'd been mentally planning to have Guy to herself as she told him about the baby. She couldn't wait to see the happiness in his eyes. Instead, those eyes snapped to hers with a brusquely questioning glance, and she had no option but to confirm the news impersonally, with a slight nod. The joy she'd been expecting to leap into his face didn't eventuate either. He looked quite...perturbed. Worried even.

Shock and dismay coursed through her. Admittedly, his initial reaction about her getting pregnant had been perturbing, but he seemed to have come round to the idea since then. He'd been extremely happy talking about the baby on Saturday night. What on earth had father and son been talking about to put Guy in such a grimly negative mood?

She battled to hide her distress as her gaze swept almost angrily over Martin Haywood. Why had he picked today to visit his son's office? Why did he have to come in here and spoil everything?

But then she noticed that the man looked far from well. Besides having lost weight, he had aged dramatically since his operation. He now looked every day of his fifty-seven years, whereas before he could have passed for mid- to late-forties.

Sympathy warred with her anger as he stood up, his eyes tired as they ran over her flushed face. 'You're looking well, Samantha,' he said wearily. 'Guy tells me you've been to the doctor. Surely there's nothing wrong, is there?'

Her eyes flicked from father to son, and Guy gave a hurried shake of his head. Clearly the news was to be secret for a while, which also filled her with dismay. Till she remembered her own parents' possible reaction. It was one thing to tell a modern girl like Lisa about an illegitimate, though planned pregnancy. Quite another to present one's close relatives with such bold news.

'Just had to get a prescription refilled,' she returned, and walked briskly into the kitchenette.

'Very efficient girl, that,' she heard Martin mutter behind her.

It was only when she removed her overcoat that Samantha remembered her clothes, the dress Guy had bought for her last Saturday morning, saying it filled his 'access' requirements. 'To be worn on Monday,' he had whispered as the saleslady had wrapped it up.

A very feminine Paisley printed dress, predominantly wine in colour, it had a scooped neck, dropped waistline, gathered skirt and tiny buttons down the front, the sort of dress designed to remind men that a woman was a woman. Not the sort of thing Martin Haywood had ever seen her wear before. Thank goodness she had a bra on and her hair up. She certainly didn't want Guy's father looking at her with suddenly knowing eyes.

'Well, Dad,' Guy was saying brusquely as she came back into the room to reclaim her chair. 'What are you going to do now? You need a housekeeper. You can't very well do everything yourself, not after such a serious operation. Why on earth did you fire her?'

Martin shrugged his own frustration. 'The damned woman was too bossy, telling me what I should be eating and drinking et cetera, et cetera, et cetera. If a man can't enjoy a cigar and a glass of port occasionally, what *can* he enjoy? Lord knows, I'm not doing much of anything else these days.'

'Good housekeepers don't grow on trees, Dad,' Guy said drily.

'Then get me a *bad* housekeeper,' Martin retorted with a bitter laugh.

Samantha had an inspiration, which was prompted by selfishness more than sympathy. She wanted Guy's father away from him. *Well* away from him.

'May I make a radical suggestion?' Samantha spoke up. 'My widowed Aunt Vonnie has a large home and enjoys the occasional house-guest. She's an ex-army nurse too. Knows all there is to know about recuperating patients. Of course, she *does* live in Newcastle. But that's no more than a two-hour drive from here on the new expressway. And she'd suit you admirably, Mr Haywood,' she added, thinking wryly of her handsome, strong-minded, eccentric aunt with her unswayable ideas on what one should and shouldn't eat. She wasn't too keen on smoking, either.

'Like me to ring her?' Samantha asked. 'See if she'd like a boarder for a while? She doesn't live far from the beach. She's a good cook, an excellent conversationalist and she simply *adores* port.'

And whisky. And gin. And vodka. Aunt Vonnie was a vegetarian, not a teetotallar.

'I don't know,' he said warily, as though sensing some sort of trap.

'Oh, go on, Dad,' his son said impatiently. 'What have you got to lose?'

Martin Haywood sighed. 'Nothing, I guess. Well, young woman, give me your aunt's phone number. I make my own plans in life. I don't let ladies do it for me.'

Aunt Vonnie will sort you out, Samantha thought when she handed the phone number over, but making a mental note to ring her aunt and warn her before Martin Haywood could. If she made him sound like a challenging and incorrigible case her aunt would not be able to resist. She was always bringing stray dogs or people home to patch up and send on their way. Besides, Aunt Vonnie had sounded lonely in her last letter. Her one and only son was off working at a copper mine in Borneo or somewhere equally remote. She could do with something to occupy her mind and time.

Once Martin Haywood left the office, Samantha glanced up at Guy from her chair, determined to put her growing doubts to rest. 'Don't you really want this baby, Guy?' she asked straight out.

'Of course I do,' he insisted, but with a frown. 'It's just that...'

'Just what?' she demanded to know.

His agitation was evident when both his hands lifted to rake through his hair. 'Let's just say I've been forgetting things lately,' he ground out harshly.

'Important things. You might think you're still in love with someone else, Sam, but that could easily change. Broken hearts do mend.'

His mouth curved into a wry grimace, his blue eyes sardonic as they flicked over her dress. 'Women have been known to fall in love with me, you know,' he drawled. 'And, from where I'm standing, you're every inch a woman. As for myself...' his lip curled scornfully in a type of self-disgust '... I'm the man I've always been. I won't change at this late stage. One way or another, if I don't stop this affair now you're going to get hurt, Sam. And I value you too much to hurt you.'

'You mean you value your secretary too much to lose her—isn't that more to the point?'

Her sharp tone brought an equally sharp look. But then his face softened to an expression of rueful resignation. 'There's that too, of course. I'm a selfish man. I always have been. I like my cake and I like to eat it too. But I've never deliberately hurt a woman and I don't intend starting now. I've always set clear and honest ground rules, just as I initially tried to do with you with this baby business. Unfortunately, we got off course somewhere...'

He squared his shoulders, tension in every line of his body. 'I think it best if we go back to our original plan, where once you conceived—as you have—our intimate relationship ends.'

For a long moment she just stared at him, her heart stopped. 'You... you don't mean that,' she choked out.

'I certainly do.'

'But... but you *like* making love to me,' she argued desperately.

His face hardened. 'I've liked making love to a *lot* of women.'

She supposed her face must have told its story, for his frustration was instant. 'For pity's sake, Sam, don't look at me like that! I'm merely bringing forward the inevitable. Don't tell me you started thinking like a typical woman, that I might ask you to marry me, that I'd settle down and give you a contented life, that I'd actually keep wanting you forever?' His laughter was harsh and ugly. 'Dear God, woman, that's a pipe-dream, and down deep you know it. I thought you had more common sense than to start caring about a bastard like me. Not to mention pride!'

She jumped up, her hand swinging to crack around his face with a vicious twang, bringing a bright red imprint on to his cheek. It shocked both of them. Samantha slumped back into her chair, stricken and ashamed.

Guy rubbed his cheek, his voice weary when he said, 'Yes, well, I dare say I deserved that. But you've merely proved my point. You're already emotionally involved to some degree. Much better all round if we go back to square one, try to re-capture what we both had once: mutual respect and friendship. It's the only way, Sam. I'm sure you'll see that in the end.'

She lifted bleak eyes. *Would* she? At the moment she couldn't see into the future at all. Dear God, how had she ever thought she could cope with this, that to have Guy even for a little while would be worth it? It hadn't been worth it if this was how she was going to feel. So cold. So wretched. So hopeless.

Guy let out a ragged sigh, and, turning, walked slowly into his office, shutting the door behind him.

Samantha just sat there. She was still sitting there half an hour later when a delivery man came into the office, carrying the hugest basket of assorted roses she had ever seen.

'Miss Peters?' he said. 'Miss Samantha Peters?'

'Y...yes?'

'Flowers for you.' He placed them on her desk with a grin and left.

For a second Samantha stared at them, her heart turning over. Surely they weren't from Guy? He had never sent a woman flowers in his life!

It suddenly occurred to her who had sent them. Norman! Dear, sweet, sensitive Norman. She opened the accompanying card with a soft smile on her face, only to have her hand tremble. The note said,

I forgot to say all the right things about the baby. I hope this makes up for some of them. The thrilled but selfish father.

The door to Guy's office opened and he came out, a pleased look appearing on his serious face when he saw the flowers. 'I thought I heard someone and hoped it was the flowers. I threatened the florist with extinction if they didn't deliver within the half-hour.'

He walked over and touched a big pink rose with gentle fingers. Samantha stared at him, an enormous lump forming in her throat, her mind whirling. She wanted to say thank you, *anything*, but she sat there totally tongue-tied, her only thought as she watched him lightly finger the velvet petals that those hands would never stroke her again, never hold her, never make her feel if not loved, then at least wanted.

'They're rather nice, aren't they?' he said, his gaze shifting from the flowers to Samantha.

She dropped her eyes. But too late. He had to have seen the tears. Even now they were spilling over and running down her cheeks, a sob catching her breath.

'Please don't, Sam,' he said, quite brokenly.

His distress jolted her and, oddly enough, it gave her a glimpse of things from his eyes. He had only wanted a child, had made what he had thought was a logical decision in her as the mother, only to be caught up in a torrid affair, half of which he couldn't possibly understand. Perhaps he *was* only trying to be a good friend to her, protecting her from future hurt, pulling back before she got in too deep.

Too deep...

A mocking smile pulled at her face as she dragged several tissues from the box on her desk. Little did he know, but she'd already drowned.

Wiping her sniffles away, she looked up apologetically. 'It's all right. *I'm* all right. Hormones, probably. It's also the first time a man has ever sent me flowers.'

'It's the first time *I've* sent flowers.'

'I know,' she said, then laughed at his surprise. 'Is there anything you don't know about me, Sam?'

'Lots, I would think. But my knowledge has expanded lately.'

'Sam! I think I've corrupted you.'

'Not you,' she said, thinking of Lisa.

His frown was swift.

'Forget it,' she muttered, then sat up straight, a bitter resolve slipping into her heart. Time to be strong, Sam. 'Well, Guy, have you got any name

ideas for our baby? I didn't want to decide on anything till I'd talked it over with you.'

It took a few moments for his frown to clear to
a slow smile. 'I don't have any preference except
that the names be indicative of their sex. I like boys
to sound like boys and girls like girls, with no
confusion.'

Samantha's heart perked up slightly with con-
centrating on their baby. 'I'll bring in a list
tomorrow for you to choose from.'

'You do that.'

'I'll have to find a proper gynaecologist too. Do
you know any?'

He grinned at her. 'Not offhand.'

She grinned back.

'You're excited, aren't you?' he said. 'About the
baby. I saw it when you walked in this morning.'

'Hopelessly,' she admitted.

His eyes were incredibly warm **as** they washed
over her. Yet, at the same time, incredibly sad. She
flinched when he bent forward and brushed her lips
with his. 'Sweet Sam,' he whispered. But then he
was gone, whirling away from her and hurrying
back into his office, closing the door firmly behind
him.

She stared after him, wide-eyed and, suddenly,
wondering.

She was still wondering when the day ended,
when she let herself into her cold, empty flat.

The phone started ringing, the jangling interrupting her revolving thoughts. She hurried across
her small living-room and snatched up the receiver.

'Yes?'

'I'm certainly glad you're home, my girl. I want
to have a few words with you.'

Samantha sank down on the chair she kept next to the phone. Oh, dear God... She'd forgotten to ring Aunt Vonnie about Mr Haywood and she sounded very cross, very cross indeed!

CHAPTER ELEVEN

'HELLO, Aunt Vonnie,' Samantha said with false brightness. 'I presume Mr Haywood rang you.'

'How clever of you to guess,' her aunt returned tartly. 'I dare say it's too much to ask that I might have been given some warning about your boss's father ringing me up out of the blue and expecting to come and live with me.'

'Yes, well, I meant to call you, but something came up and it clear went out of my mind. I *am* sorry.'

'Hmph.'

Direct apologies always disarmed Samantha's basically soft-hearted aunt. 'Besides, you sounded as if you could do with company in your last letter,' Samantha went on blithely.

'What is this? I thought I was the one doing the charity work. You make it sound as though I'm the patient!'

Samantha laughed. 'Maybe your having Mr Haywood as a house-guest for a while will kill two birds with one stone.'

'We-ll...I must admit Martin does sound interesting.'

'*Martin*?' Samantha was taken aback at such speedy informality. 'You call him Martin already?'

'What on earth would you expect me to call him?' came the huffy retort. 'Mr Haywood? We're both in our fifties, for heaven's sake. Truly, Samantha!'

'And what does he call you?'

'Veronica. He said it suits me better than Vonnie.'

Samantha was alarmed at the coy tone in her aunt's voice. 'Good grief, that old devil's charmed you already, hasn't he?'

'Not as much as his son has you, I'll warrant, Miss Prim. Do you think I haven't been able to read between the lines all these years, with a girl as attractive as you never producing a boyfriend of her own? Come on, spill the beans. You're in love with that rake of a boss of yours, aren't you?'

Samantha bit her lip. She loved her aunt but she had no intention of being bulldozed into a confession she wasn't ready for just yet. Tell her about Guy or her pregnancy and the woman would be on her doorstep in ten seconds flat.

There were many more months before people had to be told, and in less than six she would know for sure exactly what the situation with Guy was. No way could he go that long without sex. He would either come back to her, or start another affair. If the former happened the heart-stopping idea that had come to her today just might be true. If the latter...

Samantha hated to think of his taking up with another of his blondes, but there was no use putting her head in the sand and pretending it wasn't so if it was. Even if he was very discreet about it, his smoking habits would give him away.

But none of this thinking and plotting was helping matters with her intuitive aunt.

'Whatever gave you such a silly idea, Aunt Vonnie? If I were in love with Guy I'd tell you, wouldn't I? Don't I always tell you everything?'

'No.'

Samantha laughed. 'Guy and I are just good friends.' Perfectly true at that point in time.

'Piffle!'

'*Piffle*?'

'Yes, piffle! But I suppose, if you're not going to tell me, I can't browbeat it out of you. I just hope you haven't forgotten all that good advice I gave you years ago.'

'Good advice?' Suddenly Samantha remembered the packet of condoms her aunt had slipped into her bag when she'd first been headed for Sydney, not to mention all her harping on about protecting oneself against disease and other unwanted happenings.

She's going to hit the roof when I eventually tell her about the baby, Samantha groaned silently.

But, like Scarlett O'Hara, she quickly deposited that problem into the 'to be tackled some other day' area of her mind.

'Everything's fine, Auntie,' she reassured down the line.

'I hope so...'

'Did Mr Haywood mention he likes a drop of port after dinner?' Best to create a detour, Samantha thought.

'No, I don't think he did.'

'He also fancies a cigar occasionally.'

'*Does* he now?'

'He's been very ill, Auntie. He needs...coddling.'

'And you think I'm a good coddler?'

'The best.'

She could almost see the other woman smile. 'You always were a soft touch, Samantha.'

'I take after my favourite aunt.'

'Not to mention a flatterer.'

'Auntie!'

'And a little liar...'

Samantha laughed. 'Never!'

'Oh, go on with you. But mark my words, my girl. Your sins will catch up with you one day.'

They have already, believe me . . .

'Bye, love,' Aunt Vonnie said softly. 'Take care.'

Samantha's heart turned over as she said goodbye and hung up the phone. It was always nice to feel loved.

Loved . . .

Her memory shot back to that moment earlier in the day when Guy had bent and kissed her ever so softly, and that startling idea had tumbled into her mind. Could she be right? came the heart-quickening thought. Had he fallen in love with her?

It wasn't typical of him. But then, it wasn't typical of him to desire tall, well-endowed brunettes. It certainly wasn't typical of him to send flowers.

She couldn't stop her hopes soaring. Couldn't.

Perhaps he had fallen in love with her, but didn't trust his feelings lasting. Obviously he thought he would get bored with her, as he had with all his other women. He didn't understand as yet that this time there was more involved than just sex. Already they had shared the most intimate experience a man and woman could, that of making a baby together. Maybe, in time, he would come to recognise the strength of his attachment to her. All she could do was wait and hope.

Samantha followed Guy into the office the following morning—he was back to being late—a baby-name book in her hands. She had bought it from the newsagency on the way to work and had been studying it ever since.

'What about Mark for a boy?' she asked eagerly as he settled himself behind his desk and lit a cigarette. 'Or Scott? Or James?'

'Fine,' he said after his first deep drag.

Samantha looked indulgently at his obvious need of the cigarette. It was a very good sign. 'What do you mean fine?' she said. 'Which one?'

'How about all three? Mark Scott James.'

'Oh, all right.'

'And for a girl?' he prodded.

'You won't mind if it's a girl?' she asked tentatively.

'Why should I mind? I could teach a girl to fish just as well as a boy.'

'Certainly you could. My brother and I used to sit on the bank of the river at home for hours. But all we ever caught were toads,' she sighed, then smiled in fond memory. 'It was great fun, though.'

'You like fishing, Sam?' He seemed astonished.

'Love it.'

He shook his head. 'You constantly astound me.'

Her heart swelled with pleasure. 'OK, girls' names. I've picked out Natalie. Or maybe Violet?'

'Natalie,' he decided. 'Natalie Leanne Violet.'

'Oh, yes, that's lovely,' she beamed.

He looked up at her with a frowning glance. 'You're very chipper this morning.'

'Am I?'

'Yes.' His eyes narrowed suspiciously. 'Norman back on the scene?'

Surely that was jealousy in his voice. *Surely*.

'Of course not,' she said, before the full implication of his remark sank in and she felt quite annoyed. What did he think she was? Sex mad? 'Do you honestly think that I would take some other man to bed with your child growing inside me?' she flung at him crossly.

His hand stilled mid-air, his eyes dropping to the desk as he put the cigarette back down. They were quite unreadable when they lifted to her again. 'You have every right to do so,' was his very deliberate answer. 'And I have no right to object.'

It shook her. Would a man in love be so reasonable about the mother of his child bedding another man? Her heart sank to rock bottom as the truth hit. Never...

'It wouldn't feel right,' was all she could manage to say. 'I...I'd better get back to work.'

Samantha was pale by the time she sank back down behind her desk. Pale and shaking. He didn't love her. He would never love her. How could she have forgotten that he wasn't capable of such an emotion? He liked her and cared for her and didn't want to see her hurt. That was the only reason he had stopped their affair.

From that day Samantha's futile hopes were locked firmly away. And she stopped reading things into Guy's continuing smoking. It was too emotionally dangerous for her to cling to such a slender lifeline. He had probably decided not to complicate his life with an affair just now, to concentrate on their coming baby. Samantha decided she had to do the same. Having a baby was going to require a lot of strength, both mental and physical. She had never done anything in half-measures in her whole life, and she certainly wasn't going to start with motherhood.

A good gynaecologist was her first requisite. The name came from an unlikely source. Mrs Walton.

Samantha had decided it was going to be too hard to keep the news of her pregnancy from the woman

indefinitely. Neither was she going to start hiding
the child's paternity, a decision Guy whole-
heartedly agreed with.

The moment of revelation would live in her
memory forever.

'P...pregnant to Mr Haywood?' the woman had
repeated, mouth agape, eyes totally disbelieving.
'*That* Mr Haywood?' She had pointed to the inner
sanctum with a quavering finger.

Samantha had kept a straight face with difficulty. She could well appreciate the woman's
stunned reaction. Though devastatingly handsome,
Guy was the image of autocratic authority around
the office. Hard-working and just plain hard. There
was never a hint of anything but work, work, work
between boss and secretary. And, of course, during
their brief affair they had hidden their relationship,
the smouldering sexual tension between them producing what an outsider might have interpreted as
an atmosphere of charged efficiency.

'We're just good friends, Carol. Neither of us
wanted to get married, but we wanted a baby.'

This added news had knocked her for six.

'But...but...'

'I know it's an unusual arrangement,' Samantha
had reassured the stunned woman. 'But we're happy
with it. If you feel uncomfortable about the situation I suppose we could always get someone else
to help in the office...'

This had brought her to life. 'No, no! I like
working here. It's just that, among other things, I
thought you were leaving and I'd have extra work.
Oh...oh, I see, you will still be leaving, won't you?'

'Actually no, I won't be leaving work perma-
nently at all. Guy is going to buy me a small house
near by and has promised to employ someone to

help with the baby so that I can come in a few hours each day. But certainly your hours *will* increase and there will be days when you're needed full-time. Is that all right with you?'

The woman had beamed and was soon chatting happily to Samantha about pregnancy and babies, the name of a reliable gynaecologist quickly supplied. She had had three children, all boys. Twenty-three, twenty-one and eighteen now. The gynaecologist was her younger sister's, hers having since retired.

Once again Samantha had been amazed at this feeling of sisterhood between women once they opened up to each other. Before, Carol Walton had just been a woman with whom she'd worked one day a week, a shadowy figure. She soon became as good a friend as Lisa, though this time Samantha steadfastly refused to be drawn into any conversation about her briefly personal relationship with Guy.

That was taboo. She even put Lisa off asking her questions about Guy, saying it was over between them, and they were back to being nothing more than friends. She wasn't even in love with him any more.

'Oh, sure, sure,' Lisa had said in her usual cynical fashion, but had thankfully stopped pursuing the subject of any possible romantic future for Samantha and her boss.

The weeks of her pregnancy alternately dragged and flew for Samantha, depending on how she felt. To begin with she was very well, but around two months the dreaded morning sickness struck. Most mornings for the next month she arrived at the office looking decidedly pasty. Guy was most solicitous, but his attempts to get her to stay at home and rest were futile. Samantha had tried it one day and she'd been climbing the walls by noon. Besides, she discovered that she felt better once she was up and busy.

By four months she was feeling great again, if a woman could feel really great when her already decent-sized bust was bursting her bras at the seams and nothing fitted any more. Not that she was all that large as yet. She'd merely lost her waistline.

Guy took her shopping and bought her a whole new wardrobe of cleverly designed clothes that weren't maternity gear but could pass—outfits with dropped waistline and clever jackets, all made in wonderfully soft stretchy materials. Spring had arrived, and with it pretty pastels and gay florals.

Samantha felt valued and spoilt after their shopping spree.

But not loved.

Definitely not loved when the following Monday morning Guy came in without a cigarette in his hands, then didn't light one up all day.

It was the blackest day Samantha could ever remember spending. In the end she left work early, under the pretext of feeling sick, and went home and cried for hours. She didn't know who the new woman was—obviously Guy *was* going to be discreet. But Samantha knew Guy's habits too well to have any doubts.

In the coming weeks she watched and waited for him to start smoking again, but he didn't. Eventually the hurt became less sharp, since she never had to witness a svelte blonde sashaying into the office—and into his arms—but she spent many a sleepless night, thinking about what he was doing, and with whom.

By October she had hardened her heart against him, her thoughts turning towards the coming problem of breaking the news of her pregnancy to her family. She'd felt increasingly guilty for weeks about her failure to tell them, though she saw no point in upsetting them before she needed to. But the moment of confession was drawing inexorably closer.

Every Christmas she went home to Paddy's Plains for a few days, then spent the New Year with Aunt Vonnie. But not even the cleverest clothes were going to disguise the seven months she would be by then. They would have to be told before she showed up, looking like an expanding balloon.

Guy hadn't informed his father yet, either. Martin had been safely ensconced with Aunt Vonnie for just over four months now and, if her aunt's letters and phone calls were anything to go by, they got on like a house on fire. Samantha even began to suspect that there was more to their relationship than merely friendship, but who was she to point any fingers?

Besides, she couldn't really complain. Their obvious interest in each other had kept them away from Sydney for months. She had the most awful feeling that neither of them was exactly going to dance the Highland Fling when they found out what was up.

'That's quite a frown you're sporting, Sam,' Guy said as he strode into the office one October Friday morning.

She cast a steely eye over his favourite charcoal-grey suit and crisp white shirt. 'I was thinking of your father and Aunt Vonnie,' she said curtly, 'and what they were going to say when we told them.'

He stopped in front of her desk and gave her one of his unreadable looks. He was always doing that these days. She would catch him staring at her, but there was never any readable expression on his face. Frankly it was getting quite annoying. Let him stare at his latest lady-love, whoever the little blonde bitch was!

'Do you want me to ring them up and tell them?' he offered.

'No. Not yet. Let sleeping dogs lie for a while longer, I think.'

He shrugged. 'It's your decision. I wanted to tell them ages ago, if you recall.'

'Soon,' she prevaricated, and dropped her eyes to her work. Truly, the man had no right to be so damned attractive.

When he didn't move away from the front of her desk she glanced up again, and this time she knew what he was looking at. Her burgeoning breasts, straining against her dress. But he wasn't looking at them with any visible lust, she thought tartly as she saw the muscles tighten in his jaw. He was probably thinking she was getting revoltingly large and ungainly, and wondering how he could have ever stood to touch her.

Misery flared her temper. 'Pregnant women are terribly attractive, aren't they?' she said sarcastically.

His eyes lifted, a strange light dawning in them. He smiled. He actually smiled. What an insensitive sod! Samantha thought furiously.

'If you're fishing for compliments, Sam,' he drawled, 'then I suggest you try some other tack.' Still smiling, he strode off into his office.

Samantha slammed down her Biro and jumped to her feet. No...she didn't jump. She semi-lumbered to her feet. 'Fishing for compliments, am I?' she screeched after him. 'You're the last person I want compliments from, you . . . you . . .'

He appeared back in his doorway, the smile having become a wide grin. 'Want a cup of coffee, my lovely little mother? Or would you prefer I call you fatso?'

She slumped back on the chair, totally defused. 'Yes,' she pouted. 'At least it would be true.'

He walked over, stared down at her grumpy face, then shook his head. 'Incredible,' he murmured.

'Incredible what?' she sulked.

'Come on, Sam . . .' He held out his hand. 'We're going downstairs and having a cup of coffee in that coffee lounge you've grown partial to. The one with the big slabs of cheese-cake.'

She groaned. 'Temptation, get thee behind me.'

'That's my line, darling. But you can use it.'

'Darling?' She gave him a dry look. 'What's got into you this morning?'

'Lots of things. Shall we go?'

She rose slowly with a sigh. 'Are you sure you want to be seen with me?' In truth, at just over five months, she was hardly showing in the pretty pink floral dress with its dropped waistline and softly gathered skirt. With her hair down she actually looked very lovely indeed. But all Samantha could see was how her body had looked, naked, that morning.

Giving her a reproachful look, Guy walked into the kitchenette and brought back the loose white jacket that completely covered her gently rounded stomach. 'Here. Put this on and stop whingeing. Bring your handbag too. We're going for a drive afterwards.'

'A drive? Where?'

'A surprise.'

'I don't like surprises.'

'From the sound of things, you don't like anything much this morning. Just my luck. Still, I must have faith in my powers of observation and my many years of woman-watching.'

'What *are* you talking about, Guy?'

'Sam, I suggest you put the answering machine on and move it or I won't be responsible for what I do next!'

'All right, all right, I'm coming!' She threw him a puzzled glance, but he clearly wasn't going to clarify his crazy talk. 'Cheese-cake,' she muttered as he took her hand and pulled her along the corridor and into an empty lift. 'Just what I don't need . . .'

Guy threw her an exasperated look. 'Will you shut up?'

'No.' She disengaged her hand from his and folded her arms with a testy look his way. 'I feel out of sorts and I see no reason why I should suffer alone. You're responsible for this . . . this *stomach*. You should suffer too.'

That very stomach clenched tightly at the look of raw frustration that flashed across Guy's face. 'You think I'm not suffering?' he growled.

Samantha blinked, totally thrown by his reaction. 'No . . . Yes . . . Well, I . . .'

His face changed from black annoyance to one of steely resolve. 'But no longer, by God,' he muttered. 'Enough is enough!' The door of the lift whooshed back and several people started to crowd in before they had a chance to alight.

'Excuse *me*!' Guy thundered. 'My lady and I would like to get out. And, since my lady is in a delicate condition, I expect some room for our exit.'

Guy took Samantha's hand as gallantly as a knight with his adored queen and escorted her regally through the quickly parting throng.

CHAPTER TWELVE

'DID you *have* to tell them I'm pregnant?'
Samantha grumbled as she was propelled across the
foyer of the building and into the coffee lounge.

'Why not?' Guy urged her towards an empty
corner-table and settled her in a chair. 'I'm not
ashamed of it. Are you?'

She flushed. 'Of course not. It's just that...'

'I think this can wait till I've put our order in.
The waitresses here are so slow that it's a wonder
they're not working for the public service.'

Samantha watched Guy stride over to the counter
and speak to the woman behind it before returning
to sit opposite her, an oddly pensive look on his
face. That, coupled with all his cryptic comments
earlier, sent an ominous prickle running up and
down her spine.

'Is there something wrong, Guy?'

His eyes snapped to hers, then turned wry. 'I hope
not.' But he searched her face for several seconds
without saying anything. 'I'm going to ask you a
couple of questions,' he said at last, 'and I'd very
much like you to give me honest answers.'

Samantha stiffened. 'I don't make a habit of
lying.'

'I know you don't. That's what's a little
confusing.'

Her apprehension increased. What on earth was
he getting at?

'Are you still in love with that other man, the one who wouldn't marry you?'

Samantha almost died. Perhaps she should have anticipated that this question would crop up one day, but she hadn't. What to say? How to answer? Yes, I am, or no, I'm not? Why exactly was Guy asking anyway?

'Does it matter?' she prevaricated.

'Only to a degree. It won't change my course of action.'

She shook her head. 'You're talking nonsense today.'

'Not from my point of view.'

Their eyes clashed and she trembled beneath the determination in his.

'You said you'd never slept with this man you obviously imagine you still love,' he went on. 'And that your one time with Norman was instantly forgettable. Is that correct?'

'Y-es,' she admitted slowly, alarmed at where this conversation was heading.

'Would you mind, then, if I asked if any of your other lovers are still lurking about in the wings?'

'*Other* lovers?' she repeated, confused.

He frowned at her. 'There have been no other lovers?'

Her fierce blush was a full admission.

'I see . . .' For a moment he looked inordinately pleased. Then his frown returned with a rush. 'No, I don't. I don't see at *all*! You claimed you liked sex, Sam. Yet you're saying that before me there'd only been that one time with Norman? How could you possibly know you liked sex if that was the case?'

Samantha groaned silently. 'O what a tangled web we weave When first we practise to deceive!'

'I . . . You don't have to go all the way to know if

you like sex or not,' she improvised wildly. 'I've had plenty of boyfriends over the years. And we did more than just hold hands. Truly, Guy, I don't know why you're questioning me about my sex life, past or present. You yourself said it wasn't any of your business!'

'Well, I'm *making* it my business.' He suddenly scowled, clearly not pleased now with the way things were going. 'No matter what happens, I have a vested interest in the character of the mother of my child.'

Several curious faces turned their way, ears flapping.

'And what about the character of the father?' she retorted hotly. 'Like to tell me what cheap little blonde's been creeping between your sheets lately? Don't think I didn't notice you've given up smoking again. I know exactly what that means. I've been watching you do it for years!'

For a split-second he was as round-eyed as their breathless audience. Then a quiet satisfaction slid into his face. 'Jealous, Sam?' he asked softly.

'Of course not,' she huffed.

'Yes, you are,' he smiled. 'You definitely are... Come on, we're getting out of here.' He was up and dragging her on to her feet just as the waitress appeared with their coffees and cheese-cake. Guy stuffed a ten-dollar note in her uniform pocket, told her to have the coffee herself and ushered Samantha out of there, spluttering in protest.

Their exit was met with sighs of disappointment in the coffee lounge. It had been more interesting than a serial on television.

'Where are you taking me?' Samantha asked when Guy bundled her into another empty lift and pressed the button to the basement car park.

'For a drive. I told you earlier. I brought my car in today.'

'You could have let me have my morning coffee first,' she complained.

'And totally scandalise Sydney in the process? Didn't you see all the avid eavesdroppers in that place a moment ago? I thought we'd better be alone before more was said. Don't worry. I'll buy you some food on the way.'

'On the way to where?'

'Warragamba Dam.'

'*Where*?'

'Truly, Sam. Your general knowledge is pathetic sometimes. Warragamba Reservoir supplies the whole of Sydney with water. It's south-west of here, just short of the Blue Mountains. About an hour and a half's drive. I'm considering it as the site for the music video the Dambusters band wants to make here. Didn't I tell you?'

'No, you didn't tell me,' she said irritably.

'Well, now I did. I've seen it before but I want your opinion. On the drive out we'll also continue our most interesting discussion on your lurid past. I'd like to hear all about this man you supposedly love, the only man, it seems, not to succumb to your charms.'

'Why do you keep saying *supposedly* love? I *do* love him, the *rat*!' By this time they were making their way across the cold dark concrete floor of level three of the car park. Guy immediately ground to a halt, swinging round to face her. 'You *do*?' he exclaimed, undeniably shocked.

'Unfortunately, yes,' she mumbled.

'Just who is this bastard?' he demanded to know, blue eyes flashing. 'Tell me!'

She lifted a proudly stubborn face. 'I refuse to answer that on the grounds that it might incriminate me.'

For a long moment he just glared at her, eyes narrow, mouth thinned with displeasure. 'Have you been seeing him lately, Sam?' he asked in a low, threatening voice.

'I refuse to——'

His hands shot out and grabbed her, fingers biting deep into her upper arms. 'I want the truth, Sam,' he bit out. 'Have you been seeing this man, sleeping with him? Did you lie to me just now about that?'

She was startled by his vehemence. But not intimidated. 'You have no right to question me. You...' Her courage drifted away when she saw a frightening level of fury leap into his eyes.

'Goddamit, don't bandy words with me. Just tell me the truth! This is important!'

'I...I haven't been seeing or sleeping with any other man since my first night with you, Guy. No one...'

He let out a shuddering sigh and drew her into his arms. Stunned, she went. 'Thank God,' he rasped, and began stroking her hair. 'I thought as much, but just for a moment... I should have trusted my instincts...because even if you do still love that other man, Sam—and I don't believe you do—you don't love him as much as you love *me*.'

Her head jerked backwards, a cry of protest on her lips. But he quickly covered her mouth with his own, and soon she was giving credibility to his statement, a low moan echoing deep in her throat.

'*Me*,' he repeated, drawing back to touch her mouth ever so gently before kissing her again.

Samantha was in a total daze in his arms. The sound of a car horn blaring, wanting to get past where they were standing smack in the middle of the driveway, jolted her back to reality. She tried to reef out of those enclosing arms, away from that seducing mouth, but Guy would have none of it. He merely eased her out of the car's way and kept on kissing her.

'I don't want to hear any silly arguments,' he told her between kisses. 'No denials or admissions. After you've had time to think about it calmly you'll know I'm right. Meanwhile we're going to spend a relaxing day out at the dam ... then I'm going to take you back to your place ... where I'm going to make wonderfully slow love to you ...'

She gasped, both in shock *and* horror. Shock that this was actually happening, that Guy would even *want* to make love to her. And horror at the vision of his seeing her without her clothes on. 'No, no,' she cried. 'I'm fat and ugly. You couldn't possibly want to ... to ...'

He took her hand and placed it against him. 'Does that feel as though I don't want to, my sweet Sam? I've been wanting to for so long. So damned long. As for being fat and ugly ... My darling girl, I've never seen a woman look more breathtakingly beautiful than you've been looking lately.'

Samantha couldn't speak, her mind whirling, trying to grasp the truth behind these most astonishing outpourings of Guy's. She stared up at him, eyes wide and liquid with threatening tears. 'Are you saying ... that you love me?' she choked out.

The blue eyes sparkled with a hint of humour. 'Would you believe me if I said I did?'

'I ... I'm not sure ...'

His smile was warm and kind. 'I thought as much. You'll need a lot more loving before you're capable of accepting such a statement from me. A lot more...' He bent his head and lightly sipped at her mouth. Then more feverishly. Finally he forced himself to stop, holding her away from him with great reluctance. 'Oh, God, Sam, I want you so much, but I can see I must be patient. You're looking quite stunned.'

'I...I feel stunned. I...had no idea...'

That's not strictly true, came the immediate honest thought. You did have an idea... once. But then he stopped smoking and you thought...

'But haven't you been...?' Samantha bit her tongue. Violently. Don't say anything, she warned herself. Not a word. Your dream is hovering there, right within your grasp. Don't risk it.

'Yes?' he asked, a tender hand brushing her hair back from where it had fallen across one cheek.

'Nothing,' she muttered. 'Nothing. It's just that I...well, it's all so sudden, I don't know what to think.'

His smile was understanding. 'Then don't think at all. Float...'

'Float?'

'Yes... You be the sailing ship and I the sea breeze. Let me take you where I will... I won't lead you on to the rocks. I promise.'

His use of another ship analogy brought a wry smile to her mouth. 'And who is the captain of this ship, may I ask?' she murmured. 'Isn't there anyone at the wheel?'

'Love,' he whispered back.

Oh, God... She closed her eyes tight at the flood of emotion that gushed into her heart. She didn't want to believe so quickly, so naïvely. But she couldn't help herself. If there was even the slightest chance that he might love her, even for a little while, she had to take it.

'Sam? Are you all right?'

She opened her eyes and they were shining. 'Yes,' she said simply. 'Oh, yes...'

The dam was spectacular. A large concrete structure with a massive spillway, water cascading down it into the valley below. The perfect site for the Dambusters to make a video.

But Samantha didn't really care about work at that moment. Nevertheless, she let Guy rave on about his ideas for the video as he walked her across and around and through the massive structure, her eyes on his mobile mouth, her only conscious thought how much she loved this man, how much she wanted him.

The idea of his really loving her or of his wanting to make love to her in her present condition still seemed impossible, but as the day went on he convinced her with his tender touching, his desire-filled glances, his hungry kisses. By the time his car pulled up outside her block of flats shortly after four she was taut with both arousal and a nervous anticipation. It was still light, she worried. She wouldn't be able to turn the lights off, to hide her body.

Guy had not been inside her flat since their mutual friend Lana had left to marry her dress designer years ago, and was obviously surprised by the changes she'd made, remarking on her good taste as he wandered through the living-room. The furniture wasn't overly expensive, but it had been lovingly acquired over the years to give a homely, countrified flavour, with its large stuffed chairs, flowered sofa, and natural pine bookcases and tables.

'You've done wonders with this place,' he said.

'I've been able to afford to buy what I like,' she admitted. 'I have a very generous boss.'

'Have you?' he smiled back at her. 'I hope he doesn't take advantage of that fact,' he went on, coming forward to take her in his arms. 'I hope he doesn't demand payment for his generosity.'

She gave a shaky laugh, not sure if he was jesting or not. He claimed to love her, but any normal man in love would be talking of marriage by now, especially with a baby coming. Clearly, marriage still wasn't on Guy's agenda.

Samantha's mind jumped to the mystery woman he had undoubtedly been sleeping with lately, this knowledge twisting her heart with bitter jealousy. All of a sudden she knew she couldn't turn a blind eye to any more philanderings. In fact, she couldn't go to bed with Guy right now without knowing where that other woman fitted into his life.

'Guy... I've been wanting to ask you about... about that other woman, the one you've been... dating,' she said, her heart pounding nervously.

He frowned down at her for a second, then laughed.

Samantha stiffened. 'It's not a laughing matter.'

'Oh, yes, it is. Dear Sam...' He tipped up her chin with a tantalising fingertip. 'There is no other woman. I quit smoking because I read that even passive smoking was bad for a foetus. Actually, I was amazed that I could give the smoking up so easily. All I needed, it seemed, was a selfless motive.'

His eyes gleamed with a self-mocking light. 'That doesn't mean I gave up something else easily, though. Seeing you in the office every day, wanting to hold you, make love to you all the time, was sheer hell. You've no idea how much work I've been doing in the gym. I'm the fittest, most frustrated man around.'

Her heart turned over with joy at his confession. He had done without. For months. He wasn't lying. She was sure of it. 'Would...would you like a cup of coffee?' she asked, trying to ease her way out of his arms. Her skin was beginning to burn with the way he was looking down at her.

A tauntingly soft smile creased his handsome face. 'Now, Sam...you know you don't want coffee and neither do I. Come on, let's have a shower together and go to bed.'

Fear leapt into her eyes, fear of his disgust when he saw her in the nude.

'You're beautiful,' he soothed, pushing her jacket aside and smoothing a loving hand over her gently rounded belly. 'Extremely beautiful,' he repeated, hands moulding over her swollen breasts, teasing her nipples into exquisitely hard peaks.

He undressed himself slowly and seductively in front of her, his blue eyes glittering when, once totally naked, she just had to reach out and run her hands over his taut male flesh.

'You *have* been working out,' she murmured appreciatively.

He laughed sexily and led her into the bathroom, where he helped her divest herself of her clothes, kissing any remaining fears away as he did so, making her think of nothing but having him touch her everywhere.

The shower itself was an experience of supreme erotic pleasure—Guy's soap-slicked hands kneading her breasts, gently massaging her stomach, her buttocks, her thighs. Then he insisted she do the same to him. By the time he had snapped off the water and dried them both she was quivering with desire.

He took the silky green wrap that was hanging up behind the bathroom door and slipped it over her flushed skin, then carried her into her bedroom, laying her gently on her bed. 'This will never do, Sam,' he teased, looking disapprovingly at the single bed. 'Come tomorrow, you move in with me.'

'Yes,' she murmured breathlessly.

'Meanwhile, we'll have to make do, I suppose.' He parted the robe and knelt over her, bending his lips to her body.

'Yes,' she groaned, her arms lifting to cover her eyes as she began to squirm beneath his increasingly intimate kisses. 'Yes, yes, yes...'

'Want a cup of coffee?' he asked with a yawn.

She gave a voluptuous sigh and wrapped his arms more tightly around her breasts. 'Not yet. I'm too comfortable.'

'You *do* like your sex, don't you?' he whispered as he blew softly in her right ear.

She shivered, both in automatic pleasure and recoil at his words. Enough was enough, she decided. She could not let his impression of her in this regard remain unclarified. Turning carefully so that she didn't make him fall out of the bed, she pressed her lips to his chest in a loving kiss, then looked up. 'Only with you, Guy,' she insisted. 'Only with you...'

'But——'

'I lied,' she cut in firmly. 'I wanted you to keep making love to me, so I lied. I've never enjoyed sex with anyone else. Never.'

He remained silent at this and she had the sinking feeling that he didn't quite believe her. A burst of nerves rippled through her when she realised the moment had come to tell him the truth. 'You see, darling,' she said shakily, 'I've always known sex would never be any good for me unless it was with a man I loved...'

His arms tightened, and she looked straight into his narrowed eyes, hers strong and determined, despite her inner flutterings. 'You are the other man, Guy. The man I told you I loved. I've loved you for ages. That's why I resigned. I...I couldn't stand it any more. And that's why I jumped at the chance of having your baby. I would have done anything to have you make love to me. Anything. I wanted you so much.'

Samantha would never have believed it if she hadn't seen it. Tears pricked at those beautiful blue eyes. Admittedly he blinked them away quickly, but she knew what she had seen, and when he spoke his voice was thick with emotion. 'You make me feel so...proud, Sam. To inspire such devotion, such love. But I feel stupid, too, not to have noticed your worth earlier, your beauty, your desirability. I can only say I had programmed myself to give girls like you a wide berth, to take my pleasure with women who lived life in the fast lane and who wouldn't want the sort of care and commitment I didn't feel I was capable of sustaining.'

'I understand, Guy,' she said, thinking of the example of Martin Haywood. 'Truly...'

'How could you? I must have disgusted you at times.'

'I knew you were a good man. Deep down.'

His sigh was ragged. 'You've had to go deep, Sam. Very deep. But thank God you did, my loveliness,' he breathed, crushing her to him. 'For I swear to God, I do love you, with all my heart. I've loved you for months.'

She drew back to stare up at him. '*Months*?'

'I realise now that I fell for you on our first night together, but I closed my heart to it, pretended to myself I was stopping our arrangement to protect *you* against emotional involvement, when it was my own escalating feelings that were worrying me.'

'Of course,' he went on wryly, 'a certain minx wouldn't let sleeping desires lie. God, when I saw you in that red dress I wanted to rip it off and take you then and there. Then when you went out with Norman... Hell, I paced a track in my blue carpet that night. No wonder I forgot about your getting pregnant the next day. By then I was in a terrible state. All I could think about was finding a way to have you again...'

'I think I was of a similar mind,' she admitted.

Guy gave a dry chuckle. 'I even deluded myself into believing I was suffering from an acute attack of frustration, that in time I'd be cured. But the more I made love to you, the worse I got. In the end I began to believe I might be really in love. Then Dad came into the office that day, bluntly reminding me whose son I was, whose genes I had inherited. When you arrived, looking so lovely and open and innocent, I felt stricken. How could I live with myself if I hurt her, I thought, if I put her through the hell I put Jill through?'

Samantha was startled. 'Who's Jill?'

His sigh was ragged. 'A girl I thought I fell in love with when I was twenty-one. I was at uni at the time. She was older than me by a couple of years, a medical student. I was mad about her at first, but within weeks of our becoming engaged my passion was on the wane. In the end I didn't even want to make love to her at all. I had no option but to break our engagement. Jill was devastated. She even ... tried to take her own life.'

'Oh, my God, Guy,' Samantha gasped.

'Luckily she failed. But the guilt I felt! And the self-doubts. Jill was everything a man could want. Lovely, sexy, intelligent. Why *didn't* I love her? I started looking at my own father to find the answers. He supposedly loved my mother in the beginning, but all I remember are bitter arguments, claims and counter-claims of how each one only stayed together for *my* sake. Admittedly my mother was a cold woman, never showing me much love either. Even so, after her death Dad still kept falling in and out of love. He just couldn't sustain the depth of feeling, or the desire. After Jill I decided I was made out of the same mould. Yet I couldn't stomach being a deceiver, so I decided never to marry, to keep my affairs strictly physical.'

'But why always a blonde, Guy?' Samantha asked quietly.

He shrugged. 'Coincidence, really. I found that a lot of blondes suited my needs, especially the ones obsessed by their bodies and their weight. It was as though they wore a badge: "Here I am. I look fragile fluff and fun, but underneath I'm tough. I'm certainly not the type to try to commit suicide when we split up." Of course, I was selective. I only picked the ones who came on strong. Who promised, then delivered. And, to be perfectly blunt, I admired their frank approach. They never teased. I can't stand that.'

Samantha thought of his violent reaction to her teasing him and decided she would never resort to that sort of tactic with him again.

'My mother used to tease my father sometimes,' he went on bitterly. 'She was very beautiful and would use sex to get something she wanted, withholding it most of the time. My God, the fights that caused. I couldn't help hearing what was said sometimes. I was a very unhappy little boy. If it hadn't been for Dad...'

A warm light slipped into his eyes. 'Dad gave me a lot of love and approval. We were great mates always. I felt terribly sorry for him when each of his marriages busted up. He honestly thought each one would work, that it was the real thing. Of course, I can see now that he married the wrong sort of women, younger, showy, sexy types who probably wanted his money more than him. He was blind to their materialistic intentions, merely because they gave him as much sex as he wanted.'

He stopped and looked lovingly down at Samantha. 'If he'd married someone like you, someone strong and brave and giving, someone sweet and loving yet still so very sexy...'

His mouth bent to kiss her greedily, Samantha giving herself up to the pleasure of his lips and his words with a delicious shiver.

'God, I adore you,' he groaned. 'When I think of the pain I caused you I feel terrible. The day your pregnancy was confirmed I felt I had to be cruel to be kind, but in the end I couldn't stand what I saw in your eyes. I tried to make it up to you with the flowers, but I could see you were still hurt. I felt I had no option then but to retreat, to hide my confused feelings, except where I could innocently express them, such as in buying you those clothes. But all the time I kept wanting you. Only bitter experience stopped me telling you, showing you how much. I kept thinking I'd wake up one day and find I didn't want you any more.'

There was a wealth of self-mocking in his eyes. 'Then today I came in and my feelings simply refused to be deceived any longer. There you were, looking delicious but as cranky as sin, and I wanted to hold you so much, to hold you and tell you I loved you. I'd suspected for some time you felt more for me than you let on, so I decided to take action, to take our future in my hands and go for it. I vowed to make you fall in love with me if it was the last thing I did. Then, when I saw that you thought I'd been having an affair and how jealous you were, I *knew* you already loved me.'

Samantha gazed up at him, her eyes blurring. 'You talk too much,' she rasped, and pulled his mouth down on to hers.

The night was long. Filled with love-talk and love-play, warm showers, hot drinks, some food, but only the barest amount of sleep. Sleep could wait. Their need for each other couldn't.

Saturday morning brought rain. They stayed in bed all morning, not wanting to leave each other's arms. It was only when there came a tapping at the bathroom window that Samantha was forced to get up. She threw back the sheets and slipped on her silk robe.

'It's only Tom,' she said, 'The cat. Remember?'

'How well I do,' he drawled. 'That was the first sign, the one I so stupidly didn't recognise. There I was, listening to you talk on the phone, and suddenly I wanted to kill this man, Tom, who dared treat my secretary with such offhanded sexuality. As for *you*, I wanted to wring your damned neck!'

'Aah, jealousy,' she said, stroking Tom's head as she held him. He purred and moved his head around under her fingers in languorous contentment.

'You can stop that too,' Guy snapped testily. 'Save your caresses for me.'

Samantha gave his gloriously naked body sprawled out on her bed a mocking look. 'You're not going to be one of those nasty, possessive lovers, are you, Guy?'

'Lover!' he spluttered, sitting bolt upright. 'I'll have you know that——'

The front doorbell rang. Loudly and insistently.

'It'll be Lisa,' Samantha told a frowning Guy. 'She's a good friend. Lives upstairs. I'll go and give her Tom and send her on her way. Why don't you get up and get into the shower, then I'll make you breakfast?'

His eyes lit up. 'Bacon and eggs?'

'Muesli and wholemeal toast,' she returned. 'You don't want to have a heart attack, do you? I'm going to need you in the peak of condition for a few years yet.' She threw him a very sexy smile as she closed the bedroom door and walked off, one large ginger cat slung over her shoulder.

Still smiling, she opened the door to find not Lisa, but her Aunt Vonnie and Martin Haywood standing there. Their ready smiles faded as both their gazes simultaneously fastened on Samantha's rounded stomach, the slender silk robe not hiding a scrap of her advancing pregnancy. Tom chose that inopportune moment to leap for freedom and race up the stairs, probably to Lisa's. Which left Samantha without even a cat between herself and her shocked aunt.

'Oh, Samantha,' Aunt Vonnie said, clearly aghast. 'Why didn't you tell me? Martin...' She turned to her companion. 'I think perhaps I'd better go in and talk to my niece alone. She...'

It perhaps wasn't the ideal moment for Guy to stride into the living-room, a towel slung low around his hips, looking like a man who hadn't slept much the night before. 'Sam, honey, I need a razor. Where...?' His voice trailed away when his eyes clamped on their visitors.

Aunt Vonnie gave an audible gasp of shock. 'I knew it!' she said accusingly. 'I just *knew* it!'

'I wish I had,' Martin muttered darkly.

Guy, thank the lord, was the only one who was not nonplussed by the situation. 'Look, why don't you two come on in instead of standing there looking like stunned mullets? I presume you're the inimitable Aunt Vonnie?' he said, coming forward to take the flustered woman's hand and draw her inside. 'You too, Dad. And there's no need to look so appalled. Yes, it's my baby, and yes, we love each other, and yes, we're going to be married as soon as possible.'

Now it was Samantha's turn to look like a stunned mullet. Her rounded eyes blinked at Guy, who gave her a wry smile and a shrug. 'It was going to be a breakfast proposal. I just brought it forward a little. Do you mind?'

She gathered herself to come forward, eyes shining. 'No, I don't mind.' She slid an arm around his waist and hugged him, her heart filled with emotion. The man she loved...the father of her baby...her lover... And now her husband.

'What is all this?' a female voice chirped up from outside in the hallway. 'Someone die or something?'

Martin and Aunt Vonnie turned to stare with the older generation's shock at Lisa in her skin-tight jeans and outrageous purple jumper.

'It's all right, Lisa,' Samantha laughed, waving at her friend. 'Come on in. We're about to have an engagement party brunch.'

'*No*!' Lisa gaped at Guy from the doorway. 'Good heavens, you hooked him at last! Look, I'll just run back upstairs and get some of the champagne we had left over from our last orgy.'

At this even Guy looked taken aback.

'It's just her way of talking,' Samantha defended as Lisa scuttled off. 'She's going to be my chief bridesmaid, so you'd better get used to her.'

'Yes, well,' Guy said drily, 'with Frankie as my best man, and you God knows how pregnant by then, this could be the wedding of the year!'

'Maybe we should go the whole hog,' Martin rejoined, 'and make it a double wedding.'

Samantha's and Guy's heads snapped round to stare at him.

He took Aunt Vonnie's hand, his expression smug. 'Veronica has finally agreed to be my bride.'

'*No*!' came their chorused exclamation.

'Oh, yes! And, believe me, it's taken some doing. She kept telling me that I didn't have a very good track record in the marriage stakes, didn't you, dear? She said we Haywood men were *rakes*! And I suppose there is some truth in that, but——'

'Speak for yourself, Dad,' Guy interrupted firmly. 'From this moment on there's only one woman for me and she's standing right beside me.' His arm enclosed Samantha with loving reassurance, and her heart turned over.

'You lot still standing gas-bagging in the doorway?' Lisa scolded, reappearing with a champagne bottle in each hand. 'Good grief, I can see you need someone to organise things around here. If it weren't for me, you know, there wouldn't even be an engagement at all!'

They all stared at her with puzzled eyes.

Her grin was mischievous. 'Well, it was my red dress, wasn't it?'

Guy looked down at Samantha, eyes reproving. But she merely smiled back at him. 'I love you,' she whispered and, when a slow smile tugged at his mouth, she kissed him.

POSTCARDS FROM EUROPE®

HARLEQUIN PRESENTS®

Hi!
Things haven't
changed much in
Portugal. In fact,
Vitor wants to pick
up where we left
off. But I simply
can't let him
discover he's the
father of my son!
Love, Ashley

Travel across Europe in 1994 with Harlequin Presents. Collect a new Postcards from Europe title each month!

Don't miss
SUDDEN FIRE
by Elizabeth Oldfield
Harlequin Presents #1676

Available in August wherever Harlequin Presents books are sold.

HPPFE8

WEDDING SONG
Vicki Lewis Thompson

Kerry Muldoon has encountered more than her share of happy brides and grooms. She and her band—the Honeymooners—play at all the wedding receptions held in romantic Eternity, Massachusetts!

Kerry longs to walk down the aisle one day— with sexy recording executive Judd Roarke. But Kerry's dreams of singing stardom threaten to tear apart the fragile fabric of their union....

WEDDING SONG, available in August from Temptation, is the third book in Harlequin's new cross-line series, **WEDDINGS, INC.** Be sure to look for the fourth book, **THE WEDDING GAMBLE,** by Muriel Jensen (Harlequin American Romance #549), coming in September.

WED3

MILLION DOLLAR SWEEPSTAKES (III)

No purchase necessary. To enter, follow the directions published. Method of entry may vary. For eligibility, entries must be received no later than March 31, 1996. No liability is assumed for printing errors, lost, late or misdirected entries. Odds of winning are determined by the number of eligible entries distributed and received. Prizewinners will be determined no later than June 30, 1996.

Sweepstakes open to residents of the U.S. (except Puerto Rico), Canada, Europe and Taiwan who are 18 years of age or older. All applicable laws and regulations apply. Sweepstakes offer void wherever prohibited by law. Values of all prizes are in U.S. currency. This sweepstakes is presented by Torstar Corp., its subsidiaries and affiliates, in conjunction with book, merchandise and/or product offerings. For a copy of the Official Rules send a self-addressed, stamped envelope (WA residents need not affix return postage) to: MILLION DOLLAR SWEEPSTAKES (III) Rules, P.O. Box 4573, Blair, NE 68009, USA.

EXTRA BONUS PRIZE DRAWING

No purchase necessary. The Extra Bonus Prize will be awarded in a random drawing to be conducted no later than 5/30/96 from among all entries received. To qualify, entries must be received by 3/31/96 and comply with published directions. Drawing open to residents of the U.S. (except Puerto Rico), Canada, Europe and Taiwan who are 18 years of age or older. All applicable laws and regulations apply; offer void wherever prohibited by law. Odds of winning are dependent upon number of eligibile entries received. Prize is valued in U.S. currency. The offer is presented by Torstar Corp., its subsidiaries and affiliates in conjunction with book, merchandise and/or product offering. For a copy of the Official Rules governing this sweepstakes, send a self-addressed, stamped envelope (WA residents need not affix return postage) to: Extra Bonus Prize Drawing Rules, P.O. Box 4590, Blair, NE 68009, USA.

SWP-H794

HARLEQUIN®

Don't miss these Harlequin favorites by some of our most distinguished authors!
And now you can receive a discount by ordering two or more titles!

HT #25525	THE PERFECT HUSBAND by Kristine Rolofson	$2.99	☐
HT #25554	LOVERS' SECRETS by Glenda Sanders	$2.99	☐
HP #11577	THE STONE PRINCESS by Robyn Donald	$2.99	☐
HP #11554	SECRET ADMIRER by Susan Napier	$2.99	☐
HR #03277	THE LADY AND THE TOMCAT by Bethany Campbell	$2.99	☐
HR #03283	FOREIGN AFFAIR by Eva Rutland	$2.99	☐
HS #70529	KEEPING CHRISTMAS by Marisa Carroll	$3.39	☐
HS #70578	THE LAST BUCCANEER by Lynn Erickson	$3.50	☐
HI #22256	THRICE FAMILIAR by Caroline Burnes	$2.99	☐
HI #22238	PRESUMED GUILTY by Tess Gerritsen	$2.99	☐
HAR #16496	OH, YOU BEAUTIFUL DOLL by Judith Arnold	$3.50	☐
HAR #16510	WED AGAIN by Elda Minger	$3.50	☐
HH #28719	RACHEL by Lynda Trent	$3.99	☐
HH #28795	PIECES OF SKY by Marianne Willman	$3.99	☐

Harlequin Promotional Titles

#97122	LINGERING SHADOWS by Penny Jordan	$5.99	☐
	(limited quantities available on certain titles)		

	AMOUNT	$
DEDUCT:	10% DISCOUNT FOR 2+ BOOKS	$
	POSTAGE & HANDLING	$
	($1.00 for one book, 50¢ for each additional)	
	APPLICABLE TAXES*	$_____
	TOTAL PAYABLE	$_____
	(check or money order—please do not send cash)	

To order, complete this form and send it, along with a check or money order for the total above, payable to Harlequin Books, to: **In the U.S.:** 3010 Walden Avenue, P.O. Box 9047, Buffalo, NY 14269-9047; **In Canada:** P.O. Box 613, Fort Erie, Ontario, L2A 5X3.

Name: _____

Address: _____ City: _____

State/Prov.: _____ Zip/Postal Code: _____

*New York residents remit applicable sales taxes.
 Canadian residents remit applicable GST and provincial taxes..

HARLEQUIN®
PRESENTS Plus

When Cyn discovers that her latest client's future groom
is Wolf Thornton, the man *she'd* once
intended to marry, she begins to dream about a
return engagement.

Laura's fiancé, Patrick, is a true romantic *and* he likes
to cook. So why is she falling in love with Josh Kern, a
man who is Patrick's complete opposite?

Fall in love with Wolf and Josh—Cyn and Laura do!

Watch for

Return Engagement by Carole Mortimer
Harlequin Presents Plus #1671

and

Falling in Love by Charlotte Lamb
Harlequin Presents Plus #1672

Harlequin Presents Plus
The best has just gotten better!

Available in August wherever Harlequin books are sold.